LEGACY

LEGACY

jessica blank

G. P. PUTNAM'S SONS

G. P. PUTNAM'S SONS
an imprint of Penguin Random House LLC
375 Hudson Street
New York, NY 10014

Library of Congress Cataloging-in-Publication Data
Names: Blank, Jessica, 1975– author.
Title: Legacy / Jessica Blank.
Description: New York, NY : G. P. Putnam's Sons, [2018]
Summary: Alison, seventeen, wanted to quietly endure senior year after
the upheaval of her brother's death, but a fight with her mother sends her
to a radical environmental group, where she finds courage and strength.
Identifiers: LCCN 2017053082 (print) | LCCN 2017061545 (ebook)
ISBN 9780698173606 (ebook) | ISBN 9780399256479 (hardcover)
Subjects: | CYAC: Coming of age—Fiction. | Death—Fiction. | Grief—Fiction |
Environmental protection—Fiction. | Forests and forestry—Fiction. | Family
problems—Fiction. | Washington (State)—Fiction.
Classification: LCC PZ7.B61313 (ebook)
LCC PZ7.B61313 Leg 2018 (print) | DDC [Fic]—dc23
LC record available at https://lccn.loc.gov/2017053082

Printed in the United States of America.
ISBN 9780399256479
1 3 5 7 9 10 8 6 4 2

Design by Dave Kopka.
Text set in Sabon LT Pro.

for Sadie

LEGACY is a work of fiction, but it's based in a very real history of brave actions led, conceived, and imagined by young people.

In the 1990s, thousands of young people gathered on the West Coast, from California to Oregon and Washington, to save old-growth forests threatened by logging. Many of them were affiliated with a group called Earth First!, which had started in 1980 as a movement dedicated to saving wilderness areas through nonviolent direct action. The people (mostly kids) involved in these actions set up camp in the woods and put their bodies on the line to slow the destruction of ancient forests, raise public awareness, and allow time for legal challenges to logging plans to make their way through the courts.

These nonviolent "forest occupations" were often conceived, imagined, and led by young people who stepped up to take immediate, collective action to fight for what they believed in. These activists were often confronted by logging companies, private security, police, and even the FBI, but they persisted, and throughout the 1990s, forest occupation successfully stopped several logging operations in old-growth forests. In 1999, after nearly fifteen years of blockades, protests, and tree sits (including a two-year sit by twenty-two-year-old Julia "Butterfly" Hill), the Headwaters Reserve was created in Northern California, protecting an ancient forest—including trees more than two thousand years old—from being clear-cut.

Mature forests once covered most of the planet—but more than 80 percent of them have been destroyed, and what's left is severely threatened. Old-growth forests—forests in their original state, free of major disturbance by humans—are vital to the survival of not only millions of plant and animal species, but of the human species itself. Old-growth forests reduce the severity of forest fires, clean the air of pollution, and—most importantly—absorb and store carbon dioxide, making them crucial to slowing climate change. And they are unbelievably beautiful—standing in the shadow of an ancient redwood or Douglas fir, it's hard not to feel like there's something much bigger than us, to have created such beauty.

The world is changing fast—so fast that it can feel like it's impossible for any of us, individually, to have much of an effect. But standing up for what we believe in—and finding others who share our vision so we can learn to work together toward a common goal—is the *only* way to make real change.

It takes courage to define what you believe in for yourself—and even more courage to raise your voice. But the beauty in the world won't survive unless we stand up for it.

Legacy is the story of one girl who learned to do that. I hope she inspires you to do the same.

My brother, Andy, pulls me downstairs and into his room. "What—?" I start to say, but "Shh," he answers, serious. I clamp my mouth shut, thinking something must be going on. He takes one look at my solemn face and bursts out laughing.

For a second I want to kick his ass for tricking me, but I can't be mad: that laugh's my favorite sound in the entire world, warm and rich, full of secrets that he's just about to tell you. Something alive, and bright, right here in stupid rainy, gray Tacoma.

He clicks the door shut behind me—"C'mere"—and I feel lucky. His room is on the bottom floor of our split-level, almost underground. Through the row of tiny windows near the ceiling you can see the moss and grass and mushrooms where the soil meets the air. It's like a lair in here: guitars, speakers, milk crates full of tapes. His walls are postered floor to ceiling: Jane's Addiction, Pearl Jam, the Led Zeppelin hermit guy dangling his lantern over the lyrics to "Stairway to Heaven." Each one of those posters is like a world, a place that I could go, a universe that Andy knows and might explain to me. I know I'm already fourteen and I'm supposed to think he's annoying, but mostly I just want to know everything he knows.

He waves me over to his navy futon couch, green eyes twinkling beneath his rust-colored stocking cap. "Dude," he says, digging under the futon. "Listen." He always calls me *dude*, or *man*, or *Allie*—nicknames, carving out a little space for me and him. Even at school. We're three years apart, so this year's the first time we've gone to the same school since I was eight. He's basically the most popular senior, and he makes sure everyone knows that I'm his sister, and suddenly I have a lot more friends than I ever did before.

Andy's, like, the perfect guy to everyone; it'd be annoying, if it wasn't just the way he actually is. Teachers love him: he gets straight A's without even trying; he's an Eagle Scout; a million girls crush out on him, but their parents like him too. None of the grown-ups know he's where the sophomore stoners go for weed, or that when he says he's at the game, he and his friends are really streaking too fast down Pearl Street, bouncing beer cans off store windows, zigzagging through flat, low concrete buildings, blazing through the cold gray wet. Or that they bring me along.

He pulls out two six-packs of Olympia, sweat beading on the blue-and-gold cans. "So check it out."

"Okay?" I say. "It's beer." Everyone at school drinks, but I've never seen the point. It just makes you talk loud and smell gross the next morning. And when I'm out with Andy and his friends, driving with the windows down, stars flashing fast like fireworks, I don't want it to be blurry. "So what."

"I graduate in June," he says. "As of then, you'll be on your own. Which means"—he pulls a can out of the plastic rings—"you've got eight months to learn to drink properly without making an ass of yourself."

I just look at him. "Beer is gross."

"You think I drink this shit 'cause it's delicious?"

I grin despite myself. "No."

"You're gonna need to know how to keep your shit together when I'm not there to look out for you." He cracks the tab.

I don't want to think about that. Most kids at our school don't go to college afterward, and the ones who do mostly stay near Tacoma. But Andy has a scholarship. To UC Santa Barbara. Which is like a thousand miles away.

"C'mon," he says. "Lemme be a good big brother."

"Fine," I groan.

"Okay," he says, starting the lesson. "So how much have you ever drunk at once?"

"I don't know," I say. "Like, a beer? Some schnapps?"

"Okay, first of all," he says, "stop drinking schnapps. That shit is embarrassing. Plus, you'll wind up with your stomach pumped." That did happen to some girl who partied behind the bleachers once; it's like a legend at our school.

"Don't worry," I tell him. "I'm not into puking peppermint."

"Good," he says. "So how many do you think you can handle? Five?"

It kind of scares me when his friends drink that much. Not that I would ever tell him that. I don't want him to think I'm scared of anything. "Why would I want to drink five beers?"

"You need to know your max. How much you can drink before you black out, get stupid. Guys can be assholes, okay? Plus, I don't want my kid sister ruining my stellar reputation in my absence." He smirks. "Go ahead," he says. "While I'm still here. Figure out your limits."

I roll my eyes, but then I crack the beer and take a sip.

"No, you gotta chug it," he says, "like this," and downs his in one gulp.

I hear our parents' feet clomp upstairs as I drink like he showed me. Cold flushes the inside of my chest; my head pounds like I ate too much ice cream. "Ow." I put my hand to my temple.

"Here." He grabs my wrist and holds a can to the inside part, where the veins are. "Diverts the blood flow." It does feel better. He turns up Pearl Jam. "You know I saw these guys in Seattle once? I was, like, a year older than you."

"Really?" It's 1994, and Pearl Jam is, like, the hugest band ever, aside from maybe Nirvana.

"They were called Mookie Blaylock then. Nobody'd ever heard of them, but Vedder was already amazing. I held up his leg when he stage-dived."

"Wow."

"Too bad they just play stadiums now, or I'd take you." He holds out another can. "Okay, next."

He downs another beer, then pops the tab on his third and we chug together. I finish before him. "You beat me!" he says. "Badass." It's nice to hear him call me that. "They better watch out—you're gonna turn out hard-core."

Then he pounds another. Then one more.

When the van pulls up in the driveway, the sun's already set. It's raining, the kind of steady wet Tacoma's famous for: moss lines the seams of our waterlogged roof, mounds of wet green straining against the black. Drops thump on Scott's sky-blue Chevy van, and when he shuts off the ignition, the windshield wipers stop midstroke.

I've known Scott since he and Andy were skinny ten-year-olds; he still has the same freckled bony frame, but man-sized now, like all of them. Scott cracks the driver's door, and I see past him to three more: Dave and Mike in the backseat, Brandon on the passenger side with a bottle of knockoff Jack Daniel's. They're all drunk.

"Alison!" Brandon slurs.

"'Sup, sis?" Scott grins at me.

Andy pulls his army jacket over his plaid flannel, tugs his stocking cap toward his bloodshot eyes. "Dude," he tells Scott, "you're drunk."

"So?" Scott laughs.

"So," Andy says, and grabs at the keys in the ignition, "scoot over." He pushes Scott toward the passenger seat, missing the keys the first time. Then he swipes again, stumbling a little. This time he catches the keys. He turns the van off, pulls the keys out, clutching them in his hand. "You aren't driving."

"What, you're better off than me?" Scott grins again, and the other guys laugh. I look at Andy, trying to calculate the difference between five beers and however much fake Jack Daniel's is gone from that bottle. I'm not that good at math.

"Whatever, man, I can hold it better," Andy says. Mike exhales weed in the backseat. "And I haven't smoked. Scoot over." Andy nudges Scott with his shoulder, swaying. Scott moves into the passenger side; Brandon ducks into the back. Andy gets in the driver's seat. Musical chairs.

"Andy, maybe you shouldn't—" I start to say, but I don't think he hears me. He settles in behind the wheel.

"Come with, Al!" Brandon hollers at me from the back. "We'll get something to eat."

Andy puts the key in the ignition.

I stand there, rain pelting my shoulder blades, wanting to say something, knowing they'd just laugh at me. Not wanting to be laughed at.

"Pancakes!" Brandon yells, sloppy.

Dave swats him: "Cheeseburgers, man."

Andy takes his stocking cap off and puts his seat belt on.

I look at our house, Mom and Dad inside, homework and TV; I look at the van, full of wind and speed and Andy's friends and Andy.

I can feel what three beers did to me; he had more. But he's done this before, every weekend, even. He knows, right? He knows what's okay.

Andy turns the key. Rain sticks my hair to my cheek. "You coming?"

His hands are too loose on the wheel. I want to tell him not to go; I want to say, *Get out: it's stupid, it's not safe.* But I know what would happen if I did: they'd laugh and Andy'd be embarrassed; he'd turn to them and say, "Sorry, man, she never really drank before. She doesn't know." And he'd be right. I don't. Time stretches, raindrops beating on the metal roof.

I finally say, "I've got a ton of algebra."

"Suit yourself," he says. "Enjoy the buzz. Good job, Al, your first real drinking." The van rumbles as he turns the key and guns the engine, his friends' too-loud laughter fading under the hum of the engine. He smiles at me through the windshield, then backs out.

It's the last time I ever see him.

I sit in fifth-period trig, digging my pencil into the soft pages of my notebook. Ms. Hudock drones on about equations and I take notes, trying to hold the abstract tangle of symbols in my brain. I hate math. All those symbols don't mean anything. All I want is something real. Something you can hold in your hands and touch. Not numbers and transcripts and grade point averages, not starting salaries or hourly wages. My mom says I have no idea how lucky I am that UCSB is letting me use Andy's scholarship, how she wrote them a letter and begged, how she never had anyone do that for her; she had to waitress her way through school when Andy was three, when she was pregnant with me. But it doesn't make me feel lucky. It just makes me feel like I'm following some path they charted out for someone else.

After fifth period, I stand at my locker, unloading pointless math books from my backpack, loading in pointless history. My locker's not decked out; no pinup boys for me. I've got a PETA bumper sticker, a mirror, and a Melvins poster, and that's it. Designed for maximum efficiency and minimum time in the halls. As I reapply my Wet n Wild #501—burgundy so dark it's almost black—Naomi Gladstone and her popular-girl acolytes cluster by Naomi's locker. Smirks turn to sneers on their painted-pink mouths when they see me. Naomi shakes her shiny blond hair and leans in to one of her girls, a short one in pegged jeans, permed hair, and Keds. Naomi whispers something in her ear, then looks at me, and they titter like a pack of tiny toy dogs.

Girls hate me; they all have, since freshman year. That's what happens when you have a "bad reputation." Even the cool-girl art chicks brush by you in the hallway with their Smiths T-shirts, fading back into the safe tangle of each other, leaving you alone to stare down the guys. It's not that I care so much what people say, not anymore. The thing I can't stand is the loneliness. People only see a story, a rumor, what their friend heard last week. They never see you. I wouldn't mind being a pariah, if it didn't make me invisible.

As I'm zipping up my backpack, a pack of varsity-jerseyed muscle barrels down the hall. Lacrosse or football, I can't really tell; all I know is that my heart starts thudding. It's weird how guys can look down on you and want to sleep with you at the same time. I should be used to it by now, but even after all this time it kind of scares me.

I look around; they're too close for me to slip away without them noticing. I brace myself. Team Naomi's voices trill up at the sight of them, hoping for their attention, wanting to be looked at. But the guys ignore them, and they stop at my locker instead.

John McDonnell looks me up and down, mean, his spiky brown hair and freckles giving him a redneck kind of edge. His friends cluster behind him; one of them elbows John. "Check it out, man; she's alone. Today might be your lucky day."

"'Sup, Alison?" another one says, a leer in his voice. Then he chuckles, deep and throaty, insinuating, like my name means something dirty.

It's not like I don't know how it got this way.

When Andy died, it wasn't just him that went away: the first three months, my mom hardly even talked, and my dad was literally trying to keep her from killing herself, so it's not like he could pay attention to me. My own friends got weird, distant, like I had some strange contagious death disease and they'd catch it if they got too close.

Andy's friends were the only ones who got it. They were in the van with him that night. So we were together in this survivors' club we never had to talk about. And they just took me in, folded me inside like I was one of them. Beers and speeding and skipped class, curfews crumpled up and tossed out windows, matted to the pavement by the rain. I was everyone's kid sister, and as long as I was there, we could pretend it never happened. I could still be safe, and they could still be strong. They clung to me, protected me like a kid clutches a teddy bear, comforting themselves by taking care of me.

Then that spring I got boobs.

I'd known Scott since I was seven. I slept with him in April, and then I slept with Dave in May. Then Brian, then Brandon, then Mike. The actual sex part was whatever; I guess I couldn't really feel it. I just liked having someone so familiar be so close. It kept me safe. Like someone bigger than me was looking out for me. I don't know what I thought would happen—that they'd all be my boyfriend, that even one of them would. I guess I thought that it would make them never leave.

That June they graduated, moved out, started to get jobs. By the end of summer they were gone, and by the time school started, everybody knew. The way people looked at me after that almost made me miss the pity.

John McDonnell starts at my Doc Martens, working his way up. His eyes linger on the holes in my jeans. "Wish that one went up higher," he says, nodding at the rip on my left thigh. He takes a step in, a full foot taller than me.

"You're an asshole," I tell him, the hard of my voice covering the flutter of my breath beneath.

His friends laugh. I cross my arms, armoring myself. Team Naomi stare daggers from ten feet away. One of them whispers: *Why is he talking to her?* Another rolls her eyes: *Why do you think?* They're jealous of me. Which is insane. If they knew the things that happened to add up to this moment, they would not be jealous. They would be so terrified they'd shut their mouths and turn back to their mirrors and put on their pale pink lipstick and go back to pretending people like me don't exist.

Wind bites my face as I speed down the hill on my bike. This is my favorite part: when you've pedaled and pedaled till your thighs burn, till you almost can't push any further, but you press on to the top and then tip over the hill and start hurtling, fast and faster, and the wind rushes your ears and bites your skin and it's so fast that you couldn't stop even if you wanted to, not even if a bus was headed toward you, not even if a person stepped into the street. It's the only time you feel unstuck, alive, breath racing in and out of your lungs, your body made of motion, like a storm or a wild animal. It's the only time you feel like you could go anywhere, be anything, or at least something more than the dead ends that have piled up in front of you, and you move so fast the air turns to a tunnel around you, a space where you could change, slip off your skin like a superhero and put on another face, another voice, another life.

Except eventually the hill bottoms out and gravity slows you down and you open your eyes and here you are, in Tacoma, the cranes at the container port towering spindly and black above Puget Sound, squat concrete buildings dingy with accumulated smog, rusty cars and mossy roofs and cheap vinyl siding curling off of crappy houses. And farther out, the strip malls: the monster Goodwill and the Quik-Mart, the Chili's and McDonald's, parking lots full of identical SUVs, cul-de-sacs full of identical houses, asphalt and plastic and endless, endless gray. On a good day you can see Mount Rainier poking its snowcapped, craggy head up in the distance, but most days it just fades into the dirty, pasty sky.

When I was a kid, my mom used to tell my dad that someday we'd have a house with a view of Mount Rainier. That would be the big prize, the sign they'd finally made it, the symbol of the perfect life she'd planned. "Just think," she'd say, "a window where you can look out and see the mountain from your living room." That was a long time ago, back when she used to imagine things. When my dad still lived with us, and Andy; when there was such a thing as "we." Now all there is is her, her pain like a heavy wool blanket laid over our house, blacking out the windows, trapping everything inside.

A year ago, when she emerged from her room for one of her brief fits of activity, she nailed up a cheap landscape painting of Mount Rainier in our entryway. Purple acrylic for the mountain, titanium white for the snow. It's covered in smudged Plexiglas, framed with fake lacquered wood. She hung it on top of a big ugly gash in the wall, angled to cover the hole. Within a week it was covered in dust, like the rest of our house.

I lean my bike against the wall in the front hallway, unlace my boots, and stare at that stupid, crappy painting, cracked plaster peeking out at the bottom, the broken wall showing through everything.

I dart down the stairs, hoping she won't hear me. She usually doesn't. Usually she's in her room, checked out, watching Maury Povich or Montel Williams or crying. At the funeral, she didn't even hug me; her face stayed buried in her hands. When we came home, she cried constantly, too raw for me to look at; she said she didn't want to live. What was I supposed to say to that? *Hey, Mom, my brother died and I don't know what the fuck to do. Could you maybe help me out here?* She couldn't even help herself.

So I just repeated what the guidance counselor told me: she was in shock, it would wear off, normalcy would return. But the months went by, her face red and wet, and it never got normal again. My dad tried to save her; I spent every night alone. One night through the door I heard my dad beg her to keep hanging on: they still had me, and wasn't that enough? She told him no. He told her he knew what she meant.

Eventually he gave up, started staying out at night, leaving me at home to pray to a god I didn't believe in that she wouldn't do something stupid and leave the world. And then his stuff got packed beneath the stairs, cardboard boxes stacked with the life we used to have, and he moved up to Edmonds. He didn't try to take me. She got so bad, he wanted to forget it all, close us up in a box he could leave behind, me and her and her pain, the memory she wouldn't let fade.

Once he left, I started living on Lean Pockets and Tater Tots, cut class with Andy's friends, stayed out way past midnight, slept with all of them. *Do what you want, Alison. I don't care.*

Invisible.

I slip into my room, click the door shut behind me, turn the lock. I have trig homework, but I don't want to do it. I could read ahead in *Beowulf*, but I've got a solid B in English, it's not going anywhere. Besides, I already got into college. Not that it was my doing, not really. My mom engineered the whole thing.

It's all she's really talked to me about in the last two years, the only thing that brought her out of her room and, however briefly, into the realm of the living. Calling UCSB, finding someone in admissions, telling them our story, writing letters about how all I want is to have the education that my brother never got, and she's a single mom now, and my dad left, we have nothing, and would they please allow me to receive his scholarship. In his honor.

UCSB's a party school, huge, full of frat guys. Andy wanted to be by the beach, sun beating bright on everything. Golden. That isn't me; it won't be, ever. But she wants me to go, so she can pretend he has some kind of legacy. And I know what'll happen if I tell her no: she'll fall apart, like I'm taking away her life, his life. Like I'm taking him from her. Again. I applied and got in.

But I also did another thing. At the guidance counselor's, where I hide sometimes from Naomi and the jocks, there are these catalogs no one ever looks at, and I found one: for

Antioch, this school in Ohio, tiny and weird, no grades, no majors. I saw the pictures, all the kids freaky-looking and different, and for some reason I imagined that school might be full of people like me, the ones who are alone because they have to be, because nobody else is strong enough to understand or help. I filled out the application secretly. I told my whole story in my essay. And I got in. It's not like I can really go: tuition costs like fifteen thousand dollars. My mom doesn't have the money; she wouldn't pay it even if she did. But there's something comforting about having something that belongs to me, something she doesn't know about, even if it's just a place I go to in my mind.

I go to the full-length mirror propped against the wall. I keep the letter folded up behind the mirror, tucked inside a notebook, where she can never see it. *Dear Alison: We are thrilled to invite you to join the Antioch community.* Reading it, two things twist inside me: the comfort of knowing someone somewhere wants me, and the knot of knowing that I can never say yes.

That knot swells till it's a dull, hot pain between my ribs. I fold the letter back up and look at the nine tiny rings lined up in my left earlobe. There's just enough room for one more. I flick my lighter and hold the flame to a safety pin till the tip glows orange, then black. I let it cool for a second, and then I stretch out my earlobe and jam it through. No ice; I like the pain. My eyes water, hot; the knot unties, my cheeks flush, and I feel like I do hurtling down that hill on my bike: for a second, alive.

I'm closing the safety pin around my ear when she knocks on my door. I don't answer. I wipe the tears from my eyes, the snot from my nose, and sit down on the rug. I screw open a tiny bottle of Wite-Out and start painting it on my fingernails, feigning calm.

"Alison?" she says, knocking again.

I don't answer. I don't want to talk to her.

"*Ali*son." She pounds on the door now—"I saw your bike; I know you're home"—and then she tries to turn the knob. I wipe a glob of Wite-Out on my jeans. My earlobe throbs, hot.

She jiggles the handle. "Is your door locked?"

Pause.

"Alison? Is this door locked?"

"I guess so."

Pause. Jiggle. Click.

"Well, could you unlock it, please?"

"My hands are kind of full."

"Alison."

"What?"

"Open the door."

"Hang on."

"*Open the door.*"

Pause.

"Fine."

I screw the clumpy cap back on the Wite-Out and unlock the door; she walks in. Her dishwater hair grazes her skinny shoulders, light denim jeans skating up her flat hips to her waist. We have the same build, long-limbed and lanky, but when Andy died, she lost her curves, and mine came in six months later. So we don't look the same. She's wearing half the made-up face she had this morning: dried lipstick rings the edges of her mouth, orange powder clings to her cheeks, mascara smudged beneath her eyes. She painted it all on before work: her mask for the world. For strangers, she tries. But not for me.

"Here." She thrusts a thick envelope out. It's heavy, like the Yellow Pages. "This came."

"What is it?" I pick at the edges, trying to keep the Wite-Out from getting smudged. She stands there watching.

"Open it."

"I'm *opening it*! Jesus."

It's the UCSB catalog. Of course: the only reason she ever talks to me.

I look up at her. "Really?"

"What do you mean, 'really'? Yes, really."

"Thanks." I pick at the Wite-Out on my nails.

She stands there like I'm supposed to do something that will make her feel different. I feel her eyes on me, wanting something I can't give her. I can't fix what's inside her. No matter how excited I pretend to be about Andy's fucking school, it will never fix her, I'll never be him. I'll always fail.

"You could at least act appreciative."

"I said thanks."

"Alison." She just stares at me.

"What."

"Do you have any idea how hard I worked to set this up for you? You're going to college." She looks at me like I'm supposed to suddenly say, *Oh my God, you're right, I forgot, you saved my life, thank you so much.* I don't say what I want to say, which is *I don't want to go to that stupid school.*

"Jesus, Alison, you have no idea how hard it was. You have no idea. I waited tables at that shithole for years so I could get a degree and a real job—"

"What, in your stupid shipping company's office, filing papers?" I picture the office she works in, its tan carpets and beige-painted cabinets, its metal desk. Piles of papers tracking imports and exports, meaningless inanimate objects passed back and forth between anonymous companies, the numbers on her charts a brittle, empty shell around the void underneath. "That's what I'm supposed to want?"

"You know, Alison, your brother never talked that way to me." Her voice is sharp, like she's jabbing it at me, poking me with it: *You're not him. You aren't good enough.*

"Trust me, I know," I tell her. "He was perfect. And he'd be excited for this stupid catalog and throw his arms around you and say, *Oh my God, thank you so much for bringing this to me* and you'd be proud and everything would be perfect if I was him but I'm not, okay? I'm not him." That knot between my ribs is back again, hot and tight and growing, and I wish I could say what goes beyond those words: *and it's all my fault,*

I didn't stop him, and I know you think that if I do what he was supposed to do, it'll close some kind of circle, but it never will, it'll never get better, I broke it, it's broken, and nothing I ever do can ever put it back together, so stop fucking asking me to, stop asking me to fix it. My cheeks burn and I feel like something wants to explode.

I throw the catalog at her feet.

It lands face-first, half open, spine split. The pages crumple. She doesn't say anything. She just bends to pick it up, to smooth the crushed corners: careful with it, gentle, slow. I wonder what it would have felt like if she'd looked at me like that three years ago. If she'd touched me the way she's touching that stupid catalog, trying to put things back together. My eyes well up. For a second I imagine her looking up at me that way: like she cares.

But she doesn't. She keeps her eyes down on the book and turns to leave.

"She's an asshole," I say into the phone. "Come get me."

"Fighting with the Man again, huh?"

"Or the Woman."

"Right, right. But can a woman be the Man, though? See, I don't know, 'cause the dynamics of authority—"

"Shut up, Jeff," I say, and laugh, grateful for the fact that he can talk about it all like it's some abstraction.

He laughs back. "Okay. I'll be there in a minute. Cool?"

"Cool," I say, and we hang up.

I've been with Jeff since before rainy season started, the beginning of October. He's nineteen. We met at Point Defiance Park; I was riding my bike and he was eating lentil mush with a bunch of punk kids near a sign that said "Food Not Bombs." It had a picture of a hand clutching a carrot like a weapon. Jeff came up while I was catching my breath and offered me some food from the big communal vat.

I waved off the food; it reeked of cumin and looked gross. But I kept my eyes on him. "Thanks, though," I said, trying to keep him there so he'd sit down. He had a lip ring and a black hoodie with a canvas patch of a bomb stitched to the back, blond spiky hair and a skinny body, razor cheekbones. Super cute.

He did. Sit down. And smiled. The first person in practically two years who'd come up to talk to me, and not to give me shit. "Tacoma's bullshit, huh?" he said.

"Yeah." I smiled back.

"That's why I got outta here." He ran his hand through his hair. His hands looked strong. "I dropped out my junior year, a couple years ago. Got my GED, though. Wanted to go to Evergreen State, y'know?"

I didn't know, but I nodded.

"Yeah," he said, shoving lentil mush into his mouth. He pushed his lip ring aside with his tongue. "Evergreen wasn't as cool as I thought it'd be." I traced the tribal tattoos on his arms with my eyes. "It's supposed to be this alternative college, which I thought meant they would actually present some kind of actual *alternative* to the capitalist lifestyle. No such fuckin' luck, man." He was nothing like the guys at school.

"Yeah, well," I stalled, trying to think of something to say that would make him think I was as fascinating as he was to me, with his tattoos and piercings and blue eyes that were different from anyone I'd ever seen. The best I could come up with was "Everybody's gotta go to the mall, right?"

He squinted at me, wondering if I was serious, and I squirmed under his punk-rock gaze. I was about to backtrack, pull the uncool move of explaining I didn't *really* think everyone should go to the mall, when he realized I was being sarcastic.

He laughed. "Totally," he said, and my shoulders dropped. "Once I moved into the dorms, I realized it was just a bunch of hippies wearing too much corduroy and playing hacky sack. I couldn't hang with people who just got high and sat around philosophizing, y'know?"

"Yeah," I laughed, fake-brave, like I knew exactly what he was talking about. "I guess it's easier to talk about things than to do them."

"Damn right." He looked at me, something like respect in his eyes.

Nobody'd looked at me like that since Andy.

"So what'd you do?" I leaned up against a tree, bark rough against my back, trying to look comfortable.

"I dropped out, man. Fuck hippies. Laziness is just another form of conformity, y'know? I moved back up here a couple months ago. I'm crashing in my dad's basement till I can find a squat or something."

My mom would hate him. Which I loved.

"I've got a band with some guys. One of them's in Portland, the other's in Seattle, so our gigs are, like, on hold for the moment, but we're getting a house in Portland next year, and then we're gonna let it rip. I play bass." He paused meaningfully after the bass thing, like he knew it would impress me.

"So what about you, Alison?" he said. "What's your deal?"

"I don't know," I said, on the spot. "I go to school?"

"What else?" he said, his eyes on me, steady, like he actually cared.

"I hate my mom?" I said.

"Good." He nodded. "Not afraid to speak the truth."

"Wouldn't do any good not to, right?"

And then he gave me this look, one that said, *I know you, fellow outsider: we're on the same team.* It was like he saw me as a person—not a little kid, not Andy's sister, not a piece of meat. Just me. I'd never had a guy look at me like that before. Especially not one who looked like him. This guy had something for me, something different from my mom, the lonely empty hole of school. If I could have him, maybe I could have a self away from that.

We sat like that all afternoon, staring out at the Sound, leaned up against the oak tree, trash mixing with grass at our feet. We sat until the Food Not Bombs kids packed up and he hollered to them, "Catch you later," till the sky dimmed and the sun began to set. He didn't see a story someone told, a history that preceded me, a reputation or a tragedy. He told me stories about places that weren't here and assumed I'd understand them. I hadn't heard of any of it—punk shows, autonomous zones, collective houses—but he didn't care. I wanted to know everything. I wanted him to take me there someday, to places full of people I'd never met before, who did things and said what they meant and were alive.

Now I hear a rap on my window, sharp and tinny against the thin glass. I listen for my mom upstairs: nothing. She's asleep. Jeff's lip ring glints in the reflected light from my room. I hold my finger up—*one sec*—and he nods. He darts out of the light, stealthy like a ferret or a criminal, heads back toward his car parked halfway down the block, where he always waits for me. I finish lacing up my boots and pull a sweater on.

"Hurry up, man," he says as I climb into the passenger seat of Grandpa. As in, "grandpa car": American-made, big seats, big trunk, big wheels. It's from, like, 1980. The peeling navy-blue paint doesn't show much dirt, which is good, because Jeff's not much of a washer. His faded black hoodie says "Eat the Rich." He leans over and kisses me. His scruff rubs against my cheek, sexy and male. His cigarette breath makes me crave one.

He reads my mind, shaking out a half-crushed American Spirit, flipping open his Zippo. "Here," he goes. "Knock yourself out." He starts the ignition and switches on the radio. I roll down my window; I don't care if it's raining. I lean out into the asphalt-black night.

"Hey," he says. Rain hits my closed eyes, my cheeks, my tongue. One of his crazytown talk shows is playing on the radio: some guy getting super intense about how the government is hiding information about aliens. "I'm trying to listen."

"So?" I ask, turning my head back into the car. I'm a little curious about the aliens, but I'd rather feel the air.

"So," he says, "I don't want all of eastern Tacoma to hear."

I smile and shake my head. Jeff loves to act like he's in a spy movie. Like the government is following him, or weird men in black suits. He uses words like *shadow government*, *Illuminati*, and *security culture*, and says it's crucial not to let strangers know too much about your personal business. You never know who might be listening; you never know who people really are. I think it's funny that he thinks he's that important. We're a couple of kids in Tacoma, Washington; the FBI has better things to do than follow us for listening to the radio.

We drive to the parking lot at Wilson High, park away from the floodlights, tucked into a dark-shadowed corner. Our own little world, no one else around. He pulls out a bowl. This is what we do: drive to places where there's good reception, smoke pot, make out while people call in with fantasies of secret weapons systems testing and CIA mind control. The soundtrack might be weird, but I don't care: this is the only thing I have that's mine.

Jeff's crazytown talk show goes staticky and he fusses

with the radio, trying to tune back in the AM frequency at the bottom of the dial. "Shit." It doesn't work. He keeps fiddling. "Fuckin' piece-of-shit car—" It still doesn't work. "Crap!" He gives up, flipping the station to KAOS 89.3, the Evergreen State station. According to Jeff, it's the only thing about Evergreen that's truly subversive, even if some of the shows play cheesy world music with didgeridoos.

The didgeridoos mix with trip-hop beats, then sitars, and I finally say, "Do we have to listen to this?" but Jeff cuts me off. "Shh. It's almost Independent World News," and sure enough, right then the tabla drums fade and a conspiratorial voice comes on.

"Good evening, and welcome to the only truly independent news feed for the people. This just in today: Cascade Lumber has allegedly inked a deal with the Bureau of Land Management to purchase one thousand acres of pristine old-growth in the Chinook Pass Wilderness Area. Next up, a long-awaited update on the case of American political prisoner Mumia Abu-Jamal . . ."

I roll the windows down again. The smoke is getting to me; I want to feel the air. "Hey!" he stage-whispers.

"What?" I say. "The men in black can't hear it if I turn it down," and I do. He starts to argue, but I lean in to kiss him, his metal lip ring cool against my tongue, knowing it'll shut him up and make me feel alive.

CHAPTER 2

On my way in from school, I stop my bike by the mailbox. No car in the driveway: my mom's still at work. The envelopes are soggy; leafing through, I try not to tear them. Gas bill for my mom. Craft-supply catalog, also for mom. An envelope from the Boy Scouts of America, addressed to both my parents. Shit. I tear it open: *You know the joy and rewards of having a son grow up in Scouts. Now help us pass on that opportunity to other children.* I rip it up, then crumple the pieces, stuff them in my pocket and remind myself to bury them carefully in the trash can in my room, tuck the pieces under food wrappers and old homework, where she can never see them.

I also find a letter from school, informing my mother I'm going to LC first-period chemistry this semester if I miss any more labs. Which could affect my ability to graduate. And they appreciate her prompt attention to this serious issue. Shit.

LC stands for "lose credit," and it really doesn't seem fair: no matter how good your grades are, five unexcused absences and you don't get credit for the whole semester. I do my homework for that class. It doesn't seem right that getting coffee with my boyfriend in the morning would be that huge of a deal.

But there it is, right there on the letter, *affect her ability to graduate*, and my heart starts beating harder, my cheeks pink thinking about what Andy would say to that. He always wanted me to do well. *It's a no-brainer, Al*, he'd say. *You get decent grades, you can get out of Tacoma and go where you want. That's all it is: a means to an end. Do your homework so you can go do better stuff.* That's what I've been doing, all this time: what he told me. Even though I have no idea what my "end" is, what "better stuff" I'm headed for, I've been holding on to his advice, trying to show him that I'm doing what he wanted me to do, trying to make him proud. I stuff the letter in my pocket and make a mental promise: on time, every day, now till the end of the semester.

When I get in the door, the phone's ringing. I dart into my room to answer it, wet boots leaving prints on the ratty rug.

"Dude, where were you?" It's Jeff.

"I was at school. Where do you think I was?"

"Oh. Right." Sometimes I think he forgets I go to school. "I was just psyched 'cause this buddy of mine showed up and I wanted you to meet him." I have a feeling I know what's coming next. "We were kinda hungry. . . ."

I worked this summer at a Northwest's Best Coffee and saved up all my tips; without a car or any friends, I've managed to stretch it out pretty well. Jeff wants to make music instead of being part of the machine, which means he doesn't have a job, which means that when he wants to eat something that isn't in his dad's fridge or Food Not Bombs, I get a call. But it's okay. He has cheap taste, as long as it's vegan. His car gets me out of school and home; he gets the weed. Plus, when I'm with him, I feel like an actual human being, which is worth more than any of that.

"Can I pick you up?" he asks.

"Sure."

"Cool. We'll meet Dirtrat at the diner. See you in a few." He hangs up before I get a chance to ask him what kind of name "Dirtrat" is.

"Dirtrat" is apparently a name for someone who is covered in dirt and looks like a rat. Jeff and I are sitting in our usual booth at Archie's Diner when he shows up, yells "Dude! Awesome!" and slings his arm around Jeff. They do one of those handshakes with several steps, which ends in a fist bump. I can smell Dirtrat's oniony B.O. from across the table.

Dirtrat is wearing the same uniform as Jeff and the Food Not Bombs kids: Carhartt pants, black hoodie, patched-up T-shirt. But his is covered with a level of grime I've not previously encountered. The dirt on his Carhartts is thick as a coat of wax, his once-white T-shirt now an earthy shade of tan. Short white-boy dreadlocks jut from his head in all directions, zigzagging like electrical currents. I'm glad when Dirtrat sits down on Jeff's side of the booth.

Except that sitting across from him, it's hard to figure out how not to stare. He has big plugs in his earlobes, stretching the skin out farther than a human earlobe is supposed to stretch, and his face is tattooed—yes, his *face*. The tattoo's a swirl of abstract black tribal lines, like Jeff's, except instead of being on his arms it starts on his forehead and swoops down around his eye sockets, trailing off at the tops of his cheekbones. Jeff sees me staring and shoots me a silent look across the table—*Quit it*. Dirtrat sees me staring and doesn't care.

"It's a vow," he says. "A vow never to work for the Man. See, even if I get old and, like, tempted, the tattoos keep the capitalist pigs from hiring me. So it's, like, a way of keeping a promise to myself."

"Wow, that's awesome," I say. I mean, what can you say? He's basically forcing homelessness on himself and acting like that's some kind of moral act.

"Yeah," Dirtrat says, "it is," and cracks a grin. "She's all right," he says to Jeff. "You've got good taste." Gold star from Dirtrat.

Dirtrat is from Olympia. Well, he's not actually *from* Olympia, he's actually from Iowa, but he's been living in Olympia most recently. Other times he lives in Eugene, or Portland, or occasionally Arcata. He's got some buddies in Vancouver he could crash with, but he doesn't want to get into the whole deal with the border. I consider asking him what "the whole deal with the border" means, but I decide against it.

"Dirtrat and me are brothers," Jeff tells me, and something about that makes my stomach feel weird. I don't think he knows what *brothers* means. "He lived on my dorm room couch practically the whole time I was at Evergreen. He makes a mean motherfuckin' tofu scramble."

"So you guys were roommates?"

"Nah, man," Dirtrat says. "I don't do school. This man here"—arm around Jeff again—"is just a truly hard-core motherfucker, and he let a kindred spirit crash when he needed a place."

"Dirtrat was the one who convinced me to drop out and focus on my music," Jeff says. "Best decision I ever made." I'm not sure if I agree; Jeff's played four gigs since I've known him. But he keeps saying as soon as he can get to Portland next year, it'll take off. And he is pretty good; he looks at home up there on the stage with his bass, in the background, happy.

"Yeah, after I lived on Jeff's couch, I got this squat going in an old warehouse. We had events there, bands played, it was rad for a while," Dirtrat says. "This motherfucker played shows, like, every week, and was gonna create, like, a convergence space for groups that are working on, like, issues?"

"Shit people don't want at other places 'cause it's too radical," Jeff jumps in. "Like direct action around political prisoners, anti-cop action, that kind of stuff," he says. "But"—

and then he looks at Dirtrat—"the rest of the collective turned out to be kind of—I don't know. They wanted something closer to a straight-edge vibe—"

"What Jeff is trying to say is that I got myself kicked out for puking on someone's computer."

Somehow I'm not surprised.

The waitress appears above us, catching the end of the last sentence. "Can I get you kids something?" she says. She looks tired already.

"I'll just have a coffee, man," Dirtrat says. "And maybe some ice."

"No food?" the waitress asks, gunning for an excuse to kick us out.

"Nah, man," Jeff says. "He'll eat." He turns to Dirtrat. "It's on Alison," he says. "She's cool."

"Yeah?" Dirtrat turns his weaselly face to me. "You sure?"

"Yeah," I tell him, even though I don't really feel like paying for him. "I don't mind," I lie, making a mental note to take that up with Jeff later.

"Sweet!" he says, and scans the menu. "Okay, so are the hash browns vegan?"

"Excuse me?" the waitress says, shifting her weight, pen still poised to write our order. "Vegan?"

"Yeah, y'know, do they have animal products?" He turns to me. "I'll dumpster whatever, but if it's paid for, I try to go vegan."

"They're potatoes," she says.

"Right, but are they like cooked in bacon grease? Or butter?"

"They're cooked on the grill. With everything else."

Pause. "All right. Cool," Dirtrat says. "Can you just ask them to cook them in vegetable oil?"

She is clearly planning to do no such thing. "Sure."

"And maybe throw in some peppers and onions and mushrooms and stuff. Is that cool?"

This waitress is obviously going to put meat in his food. My mom used to be a waitress; I can tell. "Anything else?"

"Nah, nah, I'm good. Thanks, man."

Jeff orders the same thing Dirtrat did, and I get eggs and coffee. Even though I don't usually eat meat, I ask for bacon on the side, as a secret apology to the waitress.

I don't think it helps.

We use the rear entrance to Jeff's dad's basement, so we skip the rest of the house. Jeff says that entrance is the only thing that makes living there tolerable: because of it, nobody can watch when he comes and goes. He has autonomy.

The rickety screen door swings shut behind us as we head down the narrow staircase to Jeff's cave. Dirtrat runs his hands against the wood-paneled walls, reaching out in both directions, filling up the space. I love this basement; it's my refuge, the place where Jeff and I hide out—like home, if home were a place you liked being.

Jeff's sleeping bag is on the couch; his stuff spills out of cardboard boxes onto the floor. Clothes, boots, pamphlets that say "Profane Existence" and "Against All Tyranny," a pile of bootleg CDs with Xeroxed black-and-white hand-lettered covers, obscure punk bands I never heard of till I met him. Crass and Conflict, Christdriver and Assrash. I like the energy of them, even if they sound more like a car crash than music.

I tumble down onto the pilly brown tweed couch: familiar territory. Weeknights Jeff always wants to drive around in Grandpa, but weekends, when we have more time, I talk him into bringing me down here. It reminds me of how Andy's room used to feel, except more *mine*. I mean, it's Jeff's, but that's one step closer. I'm far away from my mom, too far for her sadness to pull at me. There's no radio, no TV, no voices except ours—not that we talk much. We listen to his music, and laugh at stuff, and we have sex. Jeff's the only guy I've slept with besides Andy's friends, and it's nothing like it was with them. It's not like the way the asshole jock guys look at me, like they're taking something. It's real, and human, and he's nice to me. And in this dead gray rainy town, it's pretty much the only time I really feel alive.

Dirtrat slings his scuzzy frame pack onto the middle of the couch, then plops down next to it. I kind of want him off the couch; it isn't his. I try to inch away from his pack without him noticing. "Dude," he says to Jeff. "You're totally set up down here."

Jeff nods, his eyes bright and cocky. It's part of what I like about him: that thing he has where he's proud of himself for doing what he does. Where everything is a decision he's made, based on ideas that he's thought about; like it's all on purpose. Like his life is something that belongs to him. I don't have that thing. "So you're good on the floor?" he asks Dirtrat. "I mean, we could take turns on the couch if you wanted—"

"Nah, nah, I'm ultra-low-maintenance," Dirtrat says. "Built for ultimate portability."

Oh. Shit. "You're staying here?" I turn to Dirtrat.

"Yeah, man, I lost my place in Olympia, so Jeff's letting me crash till I figure out what's next."

I can't lose this place that's ours, not even for a month or two; I'll go crazy. It's the only place I have. I look to Jeff, try to send him some kind of telepathic message. *You realize this means we'll never be alone?*

But I can't catch Jeff's eye. "You want a beer?" he asks Dirtrat. Jeff's dad keeps cases in the basement fridge. He knows I don't want any.

"Sure," Dirtrat says, and I decide I kind of hate him.

They chug through two six-packs before Jeff breaks out the flask, filling it from his dad's whiskey stash in the cabinet. Jeff doesn't drink much, usually, at least not around me. He knows I don't like it. Dirtrat rummages through Jeff's CDs. "Man! Resist and Exist! This is, like, a rarity. I saw these dudes at Gilman Street in like, '95." I don't know what Gilman Street is, but I've learned with punk kids it's better not to ask: not knowing means you're one of *them*, that you're part of the "machine." Jeff overlooks my lack of hard-core credentials since I'm his girlfriend and all, but I have a feeling Dirtrat wouldn't.

"Well, put it on, dude." Jeff takes the CD and presses Play on the crappy boom box. He turns the volume up to 10 and grins at me; I'm glad to have his eyes again. Jeff reaches out his hand, faking he's a gentleman, and pulls me up into an impromptu mosh pit. Jeff shouts along with the lyrics: *Who does control of your life belong to? Does it belong to them or you?* We pick up clothes from the pile and toss them at each other, thrash to the music, our own little punk show. It's stupid but it feels good. I laugh into his eyes, wild and noisy.

Then Dirtrat gets up and joins in. For a second the three of us become a crowd, a little vortex; for a second I'm one of them. Then Dirtrat edges me out with his elbows. They thrash around and around, orbiting each other, faster and stronger than I can go, their circle too tight for me to find a way in; a blur of sinewy boy muscle, testosterone, and revolt. They speed up as the music does, and I slow down, watching. The pile of clothes gets smaller and then Dirtrat starts throwing objects: beer cans, plastic plates, pots and pans. He throws his frame pack across the room, hard: it slams against the laundry sink, knocking over the hot plate and breaking a bottle.

Then he kicks over the La-Z-Boy and starts jumping up

and down on it. One of the wooden beams on the bottom of the chair breaks under his boot. It's loud. My heart beats in my ears. "Fuck!" Dirtrat yells. "That was fuckin' awesome!"

"Yeah!" Jeff hollers. Then a flurry of footsteps sounds on the ceiling above us and Jeff's face goes pale. "Shit," he says. "My dad."

He heads over to the chair and stands it up, but it doesn't look right: Dirtrat mangled it. The arm is broken too, dangling off the chair's body like a dislocated elbow. "Fuck," Jeff says, trying to put it back together, panicking. "Alison, could you help me here?"

I start to get up, but I guess not fast enough, because suddenly he yells—"*Alison!*"—like an asshole dad chewing out a little kid, a quarterback shoving a geek against a locker. He's never yelled at me before.

"Alison, get over here and help me out! Jesus!" he shouts again. My face gets hot, and a throb rises in my chest: I want to tell him, *You guys broke it; fix it yourself.* But footsteps thunder above us, and Jeff's eyes flash with fear beneath the anger, and I know I have to help.

I hustle over to the chair. It's hopelessly broken. Dirtrat picks up pieces of glass off the floor with his bare fingers. Footsteps clomp closer, and then we hear the door open.

"Dude," Jeff says to Dirtrat, and points at the bathroom, like *Go.* Dirtrat darts his eyes toward it, but it's too late. Jeff's dad is already lumbering down the stairs.

"Jeff?" Mr. Davey hollers down. He can't see us yet.

I scurry over to the boom box, switch off Resist and Exist.

"I'm fine, Dad," Jeff yells, drunk.

His dad appears at the base of the stairs. Mr. Davey is beady-eyed and fat in that doughy, indoor American way: too much car and television, too much office chair and couch. His "Huskies" T-shirt stretches across his gut.

He surveys the wreckage. His gaze lands on me—"Hello, Alison," he says cautiously—and then on Dirtrat. I see Dirtrat through Mr. Davey's eyes: the grime, the dreads, the face tattoo. I see Dirtrat see himself through Mr. Davey's eyes: worthless, lazy, throwaway. Dirtrat juts his chin out, brave or faking it, like me with the jock guys at school.

"Take a picture," Dirtrat mutters.

I make myself invisible.

"So, um, this is my friend from Olympia, Dad," Jeff says feebly. He looks half the size he did a second ago.

Mr. Davey leafs through debris, assessing the damage. Then he turns to Dirtrat. "Well, you're headed back there tonight."

"C'mon, man, Dirtrat's my friend," Jeff says. "I can't ditch him."

Mr. Davey's eyebrows lift. "Wait, *who* is your friend?"

Jeff backs up a little, realizing what he now has to repeat: "Dirtrat."

Mr. Davey looks at Dirtrat. "That's your *name*?"

Dirtrat nods almost imperceptibly.

"Uh-huh. Okay. It's time for you to go."

Jeff again, desperation creeping in: "He doesn't have a place to—"

Mr. Davey cuts him off, his voice full of hulking authority. "Not my problem."

This is the other thing me and Jeff have in common: we both have parents who don't give a shit about us. It's this weird backward thing, when the person who's supposed to take care of you is the one who hurts you most; it makes the whole world upside down so there's no one you can really trust, and most people have absolutely no idea how it feels. Sometimes the subject comes up and I can tell from Jeff's eyes he understands; we understand each other. There's a recognition there: *shit is hard.* Like we're each in this bubble that we can't break through, but we're together in the loneliness.

But he's a guy. The times I've tried to really talk about it, he mostly blows it off, makes a joke, looks out the window. So I leave it there: we both silently know how it is for each other, and knowing is just enough to make us feel a little less alone.

Mr. Davey turns to Dirtrat. "You heard me. Out."

But Jeff makes a decision. He covers the hurt, stands up straight, and says, "Fuck that, man. That's an abuse of power." He checks in with Dirtrat like, *You've got my back, right?* Dirtrat looks at the floor. I think he's thinking more about where he's gonna sleep than about sticking it to the Man.

Mr. Davey doesn't fold. "This is *my* house," he booms. "Which means I decide who's on my property."

"Who fuckin' says, man?" Jeff says, still full of bravado.

"Do you even understand the concept of property owner-ship?" Mr. Davey squints at him. It comes out condescending, like Jeff's a kid who doesn't know anything. I see hurt flicker behind Jeff's eyes, and I want to say something, but it feels impossible.

"I understand it's *bullshit*, man," Jeff says, fake-brave. I know him well enough to tell that underneath he wants to hide. But he puffs out his skinny chest. "Property is theft."

"You know what?" Mr. Davey suddenly decides. "You're so loyal? Pack your bag and go with him. Both of you get out."

Both of you. I guess my attempts at invisibility succeeded.

Panic flashes across Jeff's face. I think he realizes he took it too far. "You can't do that! You can't kick me out—I have rights!"

"Do you pay rent?"

"No, but—"

"Great, that means you don't have rights. Welcome to adulthood."

Jeff's eyes well up, but he stares at his dad, hard. I know that feeling; I have that with the jock guys. You know what they're doing is wrong, but they're bigger than you, so there's nothing you can say. "Fuck you," Jeff finally says.

Mr. Davey gets up in Jeff's face, his shoulders twice as wide, his eyes twice as mean. His cheeks are red. "Get out."

He raises his fist. He's about three times Jeff's size. My heart starts thudding in my chest.

Jeff takes a step backward. The bravado drains away; his chest sinks in and he looks like a scared kid. "But all my stuff's here." His voice is desperate. "I can't just . . ."

Mr. Davey holds his ground.

There's a long beat. Dirtrat lurks in the corner, his eyes on the floor. He doesn't say anything. I want to do something, help Jeff, but I don't know what I could do that wouldn't make it worse.

Finally Jeff starts packing up his clothes.

Mr. Davey turns to me; his face relaxes, and out of nowhere he suddenly looks like a dad instead of like a crazy person. "Jeff'll give you a ride home, okay?" he says. His voice is sticky-sweet, condescending, like *I know this isn't your fault*. It reminds me of the jocks at school, how they act friendly when what's behind it is ugly; it reminds me of my mom, how she fakes "concern about my future" when she's just trying to get me to make her feel like she's not broken. It's a lie, a painting of Mount Rainier covering a shattered wall, fake gloss covering the rot underneath. Heat rises in my stomach, churning like a mosh pit.

But I don't say anything. I just swallow it. Jeff zips his frame pack and slings it over his shoulder. "This is bullshit," he mutters as he stomps up the stairs. Dirtrat follows silently behind him, and I head up in their wake.

We cross the street to Grandpa, Jeff hunched over, a scowl darkening his face. Dirtrat slinks a few paces behind. "Keys," I tell Jeff when we get to the car. They've had six beers each and a bunch of whiskey. I'm not screwing around.

Jeff doesn't budge. "I said keys!" I snap, heat still roiling in my rib cage.

Dirtrat looks up at me, surprised. My nails dig moons into my palms. I don't want to yell at Jeff. But I'm not letting him fucking drive.

"Jeff!"

He tosses me the keys and slouches into the passenger seat, glaring back at his house through the windshield. Underneath the mad, he looks like he might cry.

Dirtrat hauls their packs into the backseat, and I get in the driver's side and turn the key.

"Thanks for having my back in there, guys," Jeff says, sarcastic. "Way to stick up to my dad."

I look at him, surprised. He's mad at me? What was I supposed to do? I grip the wheel, my knuckles white. Jeff's never been pissed off at me before. Suddenly I feel really, really alone.

Dirtrat just says, "Chill, man."

Jeff flinches.

"This is bullshit," Jeff finally says. "Where the hell am I supposed to stay?" He pounds the dashboard with his fist. "Shit." He lights a cigarette, then leans around to Dirtrat. "You know anyone in Tacoma?"

"I mean, not that we could crash with . . ."

"*No* one?" he says into the rearview mirror.

"Nah, man, Tacoma sucks. Hardly anybody lives here. But, you know . . ." Dirtrat says, thinking a minute. He peers toward the dash. "How much gas do you have?"

Jeff leans toward me to read the gauge. "Three-quarters," he says.

"Hmm," Dirtrat says, like he's got an idea. "What time is it?"

I look at my phone. "Almost ten."

"Too late to drive up now," Dirtrat says. "But in the morning . . ."

"Drive up where?" Jeff asks.

"Well, there's this thing I heard about. Near Mount Rainier? On BLM land. Cascade Lumber signed some deal to cut a bunch of old-growth, and there's a Free State starting up."

"What's a Free State?" I ask Dirtrat, suspicious. I don't quite trust him as a source for housing referrals.

"Basically when the timber companies want to cut, and people don't want to let them," Dirtrat says. "If it's illegal, or just wrong, or whatever. People set up, like, autonomous areas on the logging roads to protest."

Autonomous. That means no authority figures to boss you around. I suspect it might also mean things like puking on your roommate's computer.

Jeff stops pulling on his cigarette; his shoulders relax. "That's a good idea, man." I look at him, surprised. His eyes are still on Dirtrat. We're driving around in circles now, biding time, rain sprinkling the windshield.

"You don't have to pay or know someone or something?" I ask, skeptical. "You can just go?"

"Sure," Dirtrat says. "If you're down for the cause or whatever. They need all the bodies they can get." He leans forward toward Jeff. "We could crash there for a while; there's food and stuff. You've got a sleeping bag, right, man?"

"Not with me," Jeff says. He shoots a look back toward his dad's house.

"It's cool," Dirtrat says. "I bet there are spares up there. Or we could hit Goodwill on the way and pick up some blankets or something." Goodwill blankets: eww. "It's a good scene. We'd be taken care of."

"Yeah?" Jeff says. He stubs his cigarette out, rubs his forehead, thinking. Hope elbows the hurt out of his eyes, and then he nods. "Okay. I'm down."

My mind races and my heart starts beating fast. Did Jeff just say he's moving to the woods? He's supposed to be here, with me, stuck with his dad while I'm stuck with my mom. Am I supposed to do this without him?

"Awesome," Dirtrat says. "We gotta wait till morning, though; mountain roads are gnarly at night."

Jeff turns to me, hopeful. "We can crash at your place tonight, right?"

The whole point of Jeff is that he takes me away. I get to be someone else with him, forget everything outside of us.

If I bring them home with me, my mom will wake up; she'll come out of her room, and she'll do the things she does. And then she won't be an abstraction anymore, something to joke about or sympathize with silently; she'll be part of how he sees me. Which means all of it will. And what I am with him will get swallowed up by the black hole of the rest of my life.

"I mean, Jeff, my mom's there. I'll get in endless shit if we get caught."

He thinks a minute, then says, "You know what? Fuck that," like he's realizing something. "Who cares if you get in trouble? Just come with us tomorrow. Skip school and come up for the day. She'll cool off; I'll drive you back at night." *I'll drive you back.* He's not leaving. I exhale; my shoulders drop.

And then he leans in to me, close enough so Dirtrat can't hear. "Al, I can't go home tonight. I need a place to stay. After that we can figure it out. Okay?" He looks at me like he really needs it. Needs *me*. "Have my back?"

I look at his flinty blue eyes. I would want him to say yes, if it were me. "Okay," I say. "But keep him quiet. I don't want him waking up my fucking mom."

CHAPTER 3

I wake up in the predawn, half-light streaming through the blinds. We made it through the night without getting caught. Shadows stripe Jeff's sleeping face beside me, Dirtrat's huddled body on the floor. I watch Jeff for a minute, breathing, peaceful; then I slip out of bed, careful not to jostle him. Dirtrat snores as I tiptoe past, out the front door.

This is my favorite time: when the sun's emerging but the world isn't awake yet. When I was little and my mom would work the early shift on Saturdays, she'd wake us up, bring us to the diner, and sit plates of poached eggs in front of us while she poured coffee for the dockworkers. We'd watch the sun rise through the windows, Andy and I, smog turning the sky pink above the Sound. I remember what the roads looked like without cars, buildings without lights, no one up besides us and the early shift, the world a secret, quiet place, still and small enough to understand.

I stand in the driveway, listening. A truck hauls logs on a far-off highway; a bird flits around her nest; an engine starts up down the street. It rattles like Scott's old van did, and suddenly I remember Andy at the wheel, his beer-blurred eyes, backing down the driveway, rain splattering on the hood. I remember standing there, silent, cowardly, letting him go. *I hate myself.* I squeeze my eyes tight to shut it out and swallow hard. Down the block a door slams closed.

When I go back inside, Dirtrat's awake, scanning my room, taking stock: spiral notebooks, cheap fake-silver jewelry, shoes. Scarves draped on milk-crate bookshelves, candle-wax-dripped wine bottles. Like he's looking for things he could take. I'm glad I came in when I did.

Jeff stirs when I close the door behind me.

"Wake up," I whisper. "She'll be up soon. We gotta go."

Jeff rubs his eyes with balled fists. Dirtrat sits down to lace his boots. His eyes land on my tattered Pearl Jam poster.

"Dude, you like that band?" Dirtrat asks.

The embarrassment of mainstream music wakes Jeff up fast. He jumps in: "No, she just—"

I cut Jeff off, hard. "It's my brother's."

"Oh." Pause. "You have a brother?"

"Had." I shut him down.

I remember that notice in the mailbox, *further unexcused absences in this lab could affect her ability to graduate.* I hear Andy's voice in my head: *A means to an end, Al. The good stuff's all after, but you gotta do this to get to it.* I can ditch the day this one time, but I can't skip first-period chem. I ask Jeff to wait in the lot till first period's over, and then we'll go. Dirtrat acts like I'm pulling his teeth out with pliers, but I lean in to Jeff. "Have my back?" I ask him, and he does.

I manage to get in, get counted, sit through lab, and make it back with no jocks, no Team Naomi, no teachers catching me. When I walk out into the parking lot, it doesn't take long to spot the peeling paint and "Fuck Civilization" bumper sticker amidst the rows of shiny cars with stickers that say "Wilson Basketball" and "Go Huskies!" I duck past the rent-a-cops and head for Grandpa, avoiding anything that might slow my escape.

When I'm four feet away, I can see through the windshield: Dirtrat's smoking weed. He pulls off Jeff's blue glass bowl, not even trying to hide. I stride up and knock on the passenger window. Jeff jumps and Dirtrat slips the bowl into his pocket.

"What are you, stupid?" I say as I open the door and Dirtrat tumbles into the backseat. I point at the "Drug-Free School Zone" sign ten feet away from the car. "Can't you wait till we get on the road?" I squint at Jeff. "Can you even drive now?"

"Aw!" Dirtrat shouts to Jeff, laughing. "You win!"

Jeff turns to me. "We bet on how long it would take for you to bring that up. I said three seconds. Dirtrat said a minute." I roll my eyes. "Don't worry, I just had one hit." I don't love it, but it's not booze, and it's not a whole bowl. All it'll do is make him drive a little slower than usual. Fits with the Grandpa car, I guess.

In the backseat, Dirtrat hits the bowl again. I spot a rent-a-cop across the lot. "Can we get out of here?"

As he pulls out of the lot, Jeff pops in a Crass tape and hits Play. *Without your walls I am alive, without your walls we all survive.* I roll down the windows and let the smoke out. The wind whips my hair into my face, stinging, as we make our way toward I–5.

On the highway, Jeff speeds it up, faster than usual, and I watch the speedometer. He's worried about beating morning rush hour; I'm more stressed about the weed in the glove compartment. It hits 70. "Slow down," I tell him. "We'll be fine."

"You want to sit in yuppie traffic for two hours?" Jeff asks me.

"You want to get pulled over with weed in the car?"

"She's got a point," Dirtrat says.

Jeff slows down. Across the divider, I watch the cars inch in from the suburbs to Tacoma, people on their daily drive listening to their stereos, bodies merging with their bucket seats till the routine and the person and the highway become one. Our side is loose, fast, almost empty. We're going the opposite way.

The city thins into suburbs. We zip past a Chevron; mini-malls and plastic signs, red and blue and orange like children's toys, smooth and shiny and fake. Timber trucks swipe by us, huge logs strapped to the flatbeds. All of it is ugly. Jeff and Dirtrat yell along with Crass, their voices adding one more layer to the jangly noise, and I stay quiet, face pointed out the window, watching Tacoma fade behind me, trying not to think about my mom in our dead house, trying to forget I'll be back there tonight.

Past Enumclaw, suburbs start to give way to farmland and you can see the seams: the spots where the grass meets the pavement, asphalt striping the green earth like scars. Silos dot the horizon; trailers tuck into the few remaining stands of trees. The Crass tape clicks to an end.

"You been up to one of these before?" Jeff asks Dirtrat.

"Nah, but I know people who have."

"Yeah?" Jeff asks. I can tell he's excited by the way he sits up straight, arches his brow. "There's like, confrontations with the cops sometimes, right?"

"I think more the Forest Service. And the lumber companies. The loggers can get pretty gnarly." *Confrontations.* I wonder what he means by that.

"Right, right," Jeff says.

"Especially Cascade Lumber," Dirtrat says. "They're some nasty-ass motherfuckers. Need to get their asses kicked. Or so I've heard."

"Yeah, totally. I've heard about their shit on KAOS. On Independent World News?" Jeff mimics the DJ's hushed, conspiratorial voice. "*The only truly independent news feed for the people.*"

Dirtrat looks blank. I don't think he listens to the news.

Jeff thinks for a second. "Wait a minute. I think I heard about this thing on that show. Is this the Chinook Pass timber sale?"

"Ah—I don't really know, man."

"I think it is. They were talking about it the other night." Jeff turns to me. "Remember, Alison? We were at the lot at Wilson—"

When we're in the lot, I'm not paying attention to the radio; I'm paying attention to his hands, his voice, his eyes. "What was it?" I ask.

"They were saying how it's, like, a thousand acres of old-growth Douglas fir and there's been this whole battle over it. Cascade's starting up this big clear-cut, remember?"

This is sounding vaguely familiar. Jeff gets more excited, putting it together: "Yeah, this was the thing they were talking about. The mainstream enviros were trying to fight it in court, but of course *that* failed, and the corporates made this deal with the feds to cut the land. They were talking about it before the segment on Mumia." And now I realize why it sounds familiar: Independent World News had the story on while Jeff and I were making out.

"Jeff," I mess with him, "were you listening to the *news* while we were hooking up?" I think it's funny, but I make a face like I'm actually upset.

Jeff looks at Dirtrat for a second; I think he's trying to figure out whether it's more important to seem like a well-informed radical or a red-blooded heterosexual male. "Well, you know, we gotta be aware about the stuff they try to hide from us," he says. "I have to pay attention so I can put it in my music, pass the word on to the people." He pauses, then admits, "It *was* kinda hard to concentrate on the story, though."

I smirk at him, flirty. "Uh-huh."

Dirtrat laughs. Relieved, Jeff cracks a grin.

Twenty minutes past the last farm, right before the road slopes up into the mountains, the guys get hungry and we stop at a Quik-Mart. Good thing, too, because as I get out of the car and see the run-down trailers dotting half-wild fields around us, I'm pretty sure this convenience store is the last outpost of civilization.

When we walk in, the guy behind the counter immediately looks like he wants to kill us. He's wearing a beard and a flannel, open to show off his "Don't Tread on Me" T-shirt. His black trucker hat says "POW/MIA." A full-size American flag hangs behind the counter, dwarfing the tiny bottles of Wild Turkey and Jack Daniel's. He just keeps staring at us, hard as stone. Like we beat up his family or something. I've never been looked at like that by an adult before, not a stranger. I actually feel like he might hurt me if he could.

We fan out into the store, scanning the shelves. This place isn't like the convenience stores near Tacoma. Instead of ever-more-inventive types of snack food, the shelves are full of staples. Soup, peanut butter, canned beans, Wonder bread. People actually buy their groceries here. It seems sad.

The counter guy's beady eyes track our every move down the aisle like he's got us in the crosshairs of a rifle. Dirtrat's shoplifting skills might be legendary, but there is no way we're walking out of here with anything we haven't paid for. I fix him in my eyes and whisper, pleading, "Don't do anything dumb, okay?"

Jeff finds the snack aisle and leans over to me in front of the Doritos. "Alison," he hisses like we're hatching a secret plot. "How much cash do you have?"

I brought a couple twenties, even though Dirtrat said there'd be food at the Free State. "We've got a budget," I tell him, sounding like my mom used to when I was little and she'd take me to the grocery store. "Ten bucks."

At the counter, Jeff and Dirtrat set down a huge pile: Funyuns, dill pickle potato chips, two kinds of Doritos, and a liter of Mountain Dew. For a couple of vegans who hate the corporate machine, they sure do like junk food. I set down a Snickers. The counter guy glares at me.

"You got money to pay for all that?"

"Yeah—" I say, reaching into my wallet.

"Oh. 'Cause you look like freeloaders to me."

I mean, Dirtrat is definitely, shall we say, distinctive-looking, but I'm wearing a T-shirt and jeans. I bristle. "I have money."

"Uh-huh. Right," he says, staring me down. "You got

a job?" He looks over my shoulder at Dirtrat. "I know *you* don't."

"I had one this summer," I tell him. "I'm in school now."

"Sure," he sneers at me. "O-kay." I know he doesn't believe me, but I don't understand why. He stares at me while I un-crumple the bills, eyes full of venom. Like he expects me to hurt him. And then he stands up straighter, squaring off with us: "So. Where y'all headed?"

Jeff starts to pipe up: "There's this Fr—" but Dirtrat shushes him fast.

"My grandma lives up near Buckley," Dirtrat tells the counter guy, his eyes wide, voice innocent. "We're going to visit her."

"Uh-huh," the guy says. "Y'know, y'all better be careful up there," and then he fixes me in his burly gaze. "There's a timber sale goin' on, missy," he says, low, like it's a warning. "Watch for fallin' logs."

"What was that?" I say as we tumble into the car. My heart thunks up against my chest; I feel like I just escaped something, but I have no idea what.

"That," Dirtrat says, nodding toward the Quik-Mart, "was that." He points at the pickup parked across the lot. The sticker on the truck says, "Have a job? Thank a logger." Another one beside it has a picture of a spotted owl in the middle of a target. "Timber economy. There's nothin' else up here."

"But what did we do?" I ask. "That guy seemed like he

was ready for us to fight him or something." Jeff rips open the Funyuns, and the smell makes me nauseous; I'm that shook up.

"People who look like us come up here for one reason," Dirtrat says. "That dude knew where we were going. We're his sworn enemy."

"I'm not anybody's enemy," I say. "I mean, not someone I don't even *know*."

"Come on, Alison," Jeff says, mouth full of Funyuns. "Really?"

"No, I mean it," I say. "I'm not." It's not something I've thought about; it just comes out, clear, from a place underneath the part of me that thinks, *that guy looked the way I feel at school.* Like you've been pushed around, by everyone, all the time, till your eyes harden and your skin armors and it looks like you're the one doing the pushing. I don't want to be his enemy.

Jeff looks at me a second, and then he swallows the Funyuns. "You don't have anything that you're against? I mean, you have to stand in opposition to what you think is bullshit."

"But I don't think that guy is bullshit."

"You don't? He practically spat in your face."

"Well, yeah, he was a jerk, but I mean, I don't know . . ." I'm not sure how to explain it. "It's like he thought he needed to fight back against us."

"He does," Dirtrat says.

"Why?" I say. "I was buying Doritos. It's not like I oppose his right to exist."

"You should. He represents everything that's fucked about the system," Dirtrat says.

I don't know how to explain to him that that guy doesn't "represent" anything to me. He looks like my mom's customers at the diner when I was five. People aren't symbols; they're people. That's like Team Naomi and the jocks: people thinking I'm a reputation, a history, an idea, making me invisible. That kind of shit is how people get hurt.

"If you don't hate him, you're just stupid," Dirtrat says. "'Cause you can count on the fact that he already hates us, man. It's a war. Hippies, punks, whatever; as far as he's concerned we're all out to fuckin' destroy his livelihood and steal his house."

"He can have his stupid Quik-Mart; I don't want it," I snap at Dirtrat; he's being kind of an asshole.

Jeff jumps in, stopping Dirtrat from arguing with me. "Yeah, but that Quik-Mart is part of a system," he explains for Dirtrat. "His customers are loggers; that's where they get their money, so that's where he gets his. Everything depends on cutting down those trees. It's capitalism, man. If they can't cut, they don't have shit. And they know we're here to stop them."

I look at Jeff. *Stop them?* I'm just here to play hooky from school.

CHAPTER 4

When we head into the mountains, the driving gets slow, the road narrowing to a single lane. Every so often a huge Douglas fir towers in the middle of our path, road curving at the last minute to miss it, and I think this route must have been paved a long time ago, back before it was easy to cut down a tree. Jeff has the stereo off for once, and no one is talking. In the quiet I can suddenly hear how loud the car is. Beside me, the woods stretch out forever, dark. Evergreens drip with moss and glisten with rain, their trunks thick as buildings. They look alive.

After a while, the road plateaus and opens to two lanes; trees open to fields. Cloudless sky stretches out before us and there it is, Mount Rainier, huge and purple and craggy, white-capped, so much bigger and more real than it looks from Tacoma.

I've only been this close to the mountain one time. My

dad brought us here when I was six, the tail end of one of Andy's Scout trips. Dad decided we'd drive up to meet the troop. My mom didn't want to go: she said it was wet up there, and everything would mildew, and Andy had a ride home all set up. But my dad reminded her we'd see Andy three hours earlier if we went. Even when he was only ten, everybody wanted to be around him. Driving up, the mountain looked almost too big to be real, like something from a storybook. As we got closer, I thought that it would swallow us, but finally it was the mountain that disappeared, not us. When we met the Scouts at camp, Andy didn't want to go home: he wanted to stay outdoors. "Why don't you show us the trails you guys were on," my dad said. "Let's hike in." I remember the shape of Andy's shoulders as he ran up ahead, zigzagging through the forest, disappearing behind trees, darting out, then fading into green again.

Now the pasture closes up behind us, trees filter out the light, and we're back in the woods. Jeff looks over his shoulder. "Where next?"

"That was the last turn I had directions for," Dirtrat says.

Jeff looks worried. "What? How come?"

I check out the gas gauge. Half a tank, but still. I don't want to be lost.

"They've gotta be careful about letting out the details," Dirtrat says, eyes darting sideways. Shit. I knew following him anyplace was a bad idea.

"How are we supposed to find it, then?" Jeff looks at the gas gauge. "This sucks."

"Nah, chill, man," Dirtrat says. "We'll find it. There's a code."

We bump along the road for a long time, looking for anything that might tell us where to go. Finally we see a blue tarp tacked to a trunk beside the road, bright plastic color clashing with the forest. "Dude," Dirtrat says, triumphant. "See? A sign."

"A sign for what?" I ask.

"We're near the Free State."

Jeff still looks skeptical. "It doesn't tell me where I'm supposed to go."

Dirtrat smiles. "Sure it does. See how it's on the right side? That means the next road off to the right is the one we should take. It's a logging road. Probably not on the map."

I want to think he knows what he's talking about. The alternative—lost in the woods with no gas and a half-empty bag of Funyuns—is too scary. But I still don't quite believe him.

We take the turn, Grandpa jostling off the pavement onto gravel and mud. Another hundred yards and we see an orange rain poncho nailed to a tree on the left; sure enough, a narrower road snakes off to the left side. The trees thicken around us, no sign of humans anywhere. I'm starting to think Dirtrat's "code" doesn't exist when I see the big hand-lettered sign propped against a tree.

"CHINOOK FREE STATE" it says, red paint on plywood, circle-A anarchist sign on one corner, the letters "EF!" on another. It looks like the hand-drawn patches on Jeff's hoodies, the Xeroxed artwork on his CDs. A huge tarp stretches across the road fifteen feet above us, tied to the trunks of two trees. Laid flat in the middle, beneath the tarp, is a plank of particleboard the size of a door; behind it is a hole in the ground. We pull over and kill the engine. Up the road, I spot a few tents tucked deep into the woods. Thirty feet past those, another tarp is stretched over what looks like a makeshift kitchen—plastic buckets, a tank of kerosene, a cooler.

"Here we are, dude," Dirtrat says, victorious. "This is it."

Jeff surveys the scene, disappointment flickering in his eyes. "Where is everybody?" He's right: it looks deserted. It's weird to me that this is the big protest that the Quik-Mart guy was so upset about. I reach for the Doritos. "There's no one here."

"Guys, chill out," Dirtrat says. "They're probably just waiting to make sure we're not Forest Service. I bet they're watching us."

"We'd be able to see them," Jeff says. "Where can they hide, behind the trees?"

"Tell you what," Dirtrat says. "Get out of the car and see what happens."

Jeff gives him a look, but he takes the keys from the ignition and unlocks the door. I take off my seat belt and climb out after him.

Stretching my legs, I inhale deep; it smells like moss and dirt. The air is cool and so clean it clears my head just to breathe it.

Dirtrat crawls out from the backseat.

Still nobody.

Jeff starts to get back in the car.

Then a voice hollers out from way up by the kitchen, wary: "Who's there?"

"Friendly," Dirtrat hollers back. Branches rustle in the distance. Two figures appear: both tall, both skinny, a girl and a guy.

The girl walks a few paces ahead of him. Her dark hair's short and spiky; she's wearing a grubby wife-beater and beat-up army pants tucked into combat boots. Her nose is pierced, her arms muscled and strong. Pale freckles spill across her cheeks, blanketing her skin beneath her hazel eyes. She doesn't have on makeup, and she's beautiful in a way that's different from any magazine I've ever seen. Suddenly I want to wipe my lipstick off. When they get closer, I can see the guy, too, his tan Carhartt pants and dark green T-shirt blending in with the forest. He wears a stocking cap and a scraggly goatee. Even from here I can see his eyes are kind.

"We came up from Tacoma," Dirtrat shouts to them. Then he leans over to me and Jeff: "We gotta tell them who we are so they know we're not here to snitch them out." Jeff nods. Then Dirtrat shouts again: "I heard about y'all from Acacia and Critter in Olympia."

The woman's face lights up. "Acacia! Love her!" She picks up her pace, half jogs toward us. "How's she doing?"

"Pretty good, I guess," Dirtrat says, fists jammed in his pockets, eyes ringed by the black of his face tattoo. "Last time I saw her was at Olympia Food Not Bombs a couple weeks ago. She was cooking."

"Right, right," she says. "Cool. Acacia's an awesome woman. So powerful, right?" Dirtrat looks vaguely uncomfortable. "I'm Sage."

Up close I can see her tattoo, the outline of a tree, black branches snaking around the curve of her strong forearm. She offers her hand to shake. The guys hesitate, awkward, so I reach mine out. Her grip is strong. "Nice to see a girl up here," she says, smiling right into my eyes. It catches me off guard.

Then the guy catches up, his gait loose and calm. He stands a foot or two behind Sage, but not like he's holding back, just giving her the lead. His T-shirt says "Northwest Biocentric Conference 1994" around this intricate circular design; a tiny ponytail curls out from underneath his stocking cap. Up close I can see they're older than me, but not by much. He's twenty-one, probably; she might be Jeff's age, maybe a little more. "Hey," the guy says. "I'm Aaron."

"He doesn't have a forest name," Sage says, smiling at him. "I keep telling him that won't be safe forever, but he wants to hold out as long as he can."

"She's probably right," Aaron says to us. "But hiding

generates its own energy, y'know? I'd rather not do it unless I have to."

Jeff crosses his arms, skeptical. "You don't think you have to?"

Aaron holds his gaze. "Yeah. I think we're okay." Aaron gives Sage a tiny smile, almost imperceptible, like a secret language.

There's a weird awkward moment. I don't even know what they're talking about, hiding and fake names and whatever. Like with the guy at the Quik-Mart, I don't see what the big deal is, why everyone is acting like there's some kind of war.

I decide to act like a normal person. I hold out my hand. "Hi. I'm Alison."

Aaron turns away from Jeff and shakes my hand. His grip is softer than Sage's but still strong. "Hey. Another *A*." His relaxed warmth seems familiar somehow.

They take us on a "tour": first the kitchen, sacks of lentils and rice, plastic vats of oil, a cardboard box of salvaged veggies. Battered restaurant-size steel pots sit on the forest floor, twigs collecting on their lids. It looks kind of like the Food Not Bombs setup in the park, except for the huge jugs of drinking water lined up beneath the tarp and the fact that we're in the middle of a forest. It's not particularly appetizing, let's put it that way. I'm glad we have the Funyuns.

Aaron brings us over to a central area between the kitchen

and the tents, a big clearing with a fire pit and a guitar case and a couple of kids sitting around. One of them is reed-thin and gangly, hunched over a notebook, scribbling. He has stringy brown hair tucked beneath an army cap—the kind you see in old pictures of John Lennon, or Chairman Mao in history books—and a quiet face, like a deer. The other one is short and stocky, ruddy-cheeked with a thick red beard; he's sturdy, like a carpenter, a punk version of the union guys who work the docks back home. His forearms are crowded with india-ink tattoos, kind of like Dirtrat but less punk in his plain grimy T-shirt. They both look Jeff's age, like nineteen. "Guys, this is Alison and Dirtrat and Jeff," Aaron tells them. "They came up from Tacoma."

"Cool, cool," red-beard guy says. "I'm Nutmeg. This is Exile." He nods toward the army-cap guy.

Nobody names their kid Nutmeg. Everyone here except Aaron has weird names they clearly picked out themselves. I thought Dirtrat was just his own special kind of weirdo, but it seems like it's kind of a thing.

"Does everybody, like, choose a name here? What is that?" I ask.

Jeff flushes red: everybody's supposed to already know the secret punk-rock codes. He turns to them, explaining for me: "She knows what it is."

"No, I don't," I say, and look at him like *What are you doing?* He's acting weird, like I'm embarrassing him or something. Until yesterday, it was always just the two of us. We've

never really hung out around a bunch of people before, especially people he doesn't know, especially a bunch of punks he
wants to impress. He won't meet my eye.

"Most people choose different names, yeah," Sage answers
me, looking past Jeff, straight at me. "When the BLM sold
this land to Cascade, it became Cascade's private property, so
technically we're trespassing. They can arrest us just for being
here, so we have forest names in case a bust happens and they
try to ask us about each other."

That's kind of crazy: that it's illegal just to stand on the
dirt I'm standing on. I suddenly feel nervous. I mean, technically, it's not like I haven't broken the law; I've smoked tons
of pot, and I told a sophomore where to buy it once. But this
is different. They're not breaking the law by accident; they're
doing it on purpose, planning, thinking ahead to handcuffs
and a night in jail. I don't know who these people are. Tacoma might be hell, but I feel just a tiny bit relieved that Jeff
is driving me back tonight.

Later, people hang around the camp: Dirtrat's wandered off
somewhere; Jeff is sitting by a tree alone, smoking. Exile's
working, stacking buckets, organizing stuff; Aaron's over in
the kitchen, rinsing rice. Near the fire pit, Nutmeg picks up
a guitar with his stubby fingers and starts playing some folk
song about the spirit of the trees. It's cheesy, filled with lines
like *sing the heart of Mother Earth*.

Sage picks up a backpack full of tools and says she's going to "fortify the front lines." She puts her hand on my arm: "Wanna come with?"

I think about all that cops and jail stuff and I don't, not really, but no girl has invited me anywhere in pretty much as long as I can remember. Let alone touched me, unless you count slamming me against a locker. The girls at school all have each other, clumped up into clusters of safety and trust; they bring each other places, stay together, have each other's backs. I forgot what that felt like.

I see Jeff watching Sage and me: he looks nervous or something, like he doesn't want me to leave. He locks eyes with me. I lock eyes back. "Thanks," I tell Sage, "but I'm kind of tired. Next time?"

"Sure," she says, watching me watch him.

I head over to sit with Jeff, relieved to finally be alone with him. His back is pressed against the tree trunk; he's jiggling his foot. He hasn't said much to me since we got here. It's like he doesn't know how to act with me when it's not just us. "You okay?" I ask as I sit down, put my hand on the leg of his jeans.

He doesn't answer, just looks up at the canopy above us. I turn my face up too. Tree trunks stretch up like spires, spindly and angular, green turning to black against the bright of the sky. It's quiet here. Really quiet, the kind that lets you hear everything you're thinking.

We haven't talked about what happens after he drives me back tonight. I'm just here playing hooky; I have someplace to go home to. Jeff doesn't. And it's a long drive from here to there. My heart thrums at the bottom of my throat as I think about it. I want to ask how long he thinks he's staying, but I also don't want to hear the answer.

I don't even want to think about being in Tacoma without Jeff. It's not that I'm in love with him; we don't say that to each other, and I think if I felt it, I would know. In movies everybody always knows. But he's my only thing. The only thing I have that reminds me I'm a human being—the only person I can laugh with, the one reminder that there's a world outside the black hole of my house and the gauntlet of school hallways, the empty abstraction of homework and the endless dark lonely of my life.

If I don't go home tonight, though, my mom will lose her shit. And if I'm not at lab on Monday morning, I won't graduate. And it's stupid, but I think somehow Andy would know.

"So . . ." I say, finally breaking the silence.

"So," Jeff says back.

"What are you gonna do, do you think?"

He looks at me. "What do you mean, what am I gonna do?"

Suddenly my cheeks flush, like maybe I shouldn't have asked. I pick at the dirt.

"I mean, like, tomorrow?"

He looks down too. "Oh. Yeah." Long pause. "I don't know."

I've never had to deal with the fact that Jeff's older than me, not really. Not in any way that was a problem. I mean, he can do what he wants with his days. He can stay out late, he can drive to Seattle for band practice, but none of that has anything to do with us. I mean, he lives at home, like me. Or—he did.

"Are you gonna stay here?"

He looks at me. "I mean, I think I have to, at least for a while."

I'm scared to ask it, but more scared not to know the answer: "What's a while?"

"I mean, until I can figure something out?"

That doesn't help.

"Zach doesn't have room at his place in Seattle," he says, "and Chris is traveling. I don't have any cash, so."

And there it is: the difference between us. He's an adult now, I guess, which means it all comes down to money. I hate my mom, but I'm allowed to sleep in her house. Jeff's dad just kicked him out with nothing. That means he's really on his own.

This space between us opens up, a distance that scares me. I want to look at him and know that he feels the same things I do, that we understand each other, that we make each other less alone. I want to make us match again.

For the first time since that day at Point Defiance Park, I feel like I need something from him that he might not need from me. I need him to come back with me—but he doesn't need me to do anything. It's like Andy in the van, when I wanted him to stay but there was no way I could tell him that, no reason he would stay there just because I asked him to. And I could have gone along, I was invited, but I was too afraid to take the leap. I feel out on a limb, suddenly. Like I might get left. It's scary.

I'm trying to figure out how to stop the silence when suddenly Sage runs back into camp. She's out of breath, sweaty, and her eyes are blazing. "You guys," she says. Nutmeg puts down his guitar; Aaron comes from the kitchen. "I heard an engine."

"Shit," Exile says, his big dark eyes alert. "How far?"

"I mean, I can't hear it here yet, so we have a minute," she says, "but it sounded like it was just a little ways down the mountain."

"Did you check the dragon?" Nutmeg asks her.

"I stuck a screwdriver in; it's dry. But just that one; the other three aren't set yet."

"Shit."

"Did you hear that?" Aaron says. Sage's ears prick up like a rabbit's; everyone stays still for a second, animals in the forest. We hear an engine in the distance, gears grinding angry and loud against the still of the woods. Still far off, but getting closer.

"Shit," Aaron says. "Let's go."

The sky's almost dark when we get to the front lines. Aaron spots Dirtrat sitting in Grandpa and knocks on the window. Dirtrat opens the car door: "'Sup, man?" A cloud of pot smoke tumbles out.

"Get up," Aaron says. "Go stash your weed over there somewhere," he tells Dirtrat, pointing toward the trees. "Away from the car and off your person."

Dirtrat's about to argue, but we hear the rumble of the engine again, closer now, and Aaron says, "Go," and he does.

Sage gathers everyone around. "Okay," she says. "Here's the deal." She turns to Exile and Nutmeg. "Sorry to be repetitive, guys, we've got newbies." Then she turns to us, explaining, "We don't know who's out there. Could be nothing. It could also be the Forest Service, loggers, or the cops." The engine roars again; she tilts her head to listen. "They're definitely headed toward us, though—not toward town—and it's getting dark, so chances are they're not just hikers."

There's a thickness in the air between us; everyone huddles close. It's like when Jeff gets intense about the FBI, except instead of being kind of funny, this actually seems real. My heart pounds in my chest and adrenaline floods my fingertips, even though I have no idea what's going on.

"It's early," Exile says. "They're not even supposed to know we're out here yet."

"Yeah, well, someone in town must've tipped them off," Sage says.

"This isn't cool, man," Nutmeg says. "The space isn't secure. We've got three more dragons I've barely even started on."

"We'll have to work with what we have," Aaron says, firm.

"Look," Sage says. "We've got one. It's dry. I checked.

And the road's narrow. Even without the other three, they can't get around us unless they've got bulldozers to dig out a ditch. So we just need to figure out who's willing to lock down."

"Lock down?" Jeff asks. "What do you mean?"

"In the dragon," Sage says. Nutmeg pulls us over to the plank of particleboard laid on the ground beneath the tarp.

"Here," Nutmeg says. I stand on the board and he crouches down, showing us the hole in the ground behind it. I peer over his shoulder. Hinged to the wood, beside the hole, is an open steel door with a cutout circle in the center. Inside the hole is a deep plastic vat cemented in the ground with concrete. At the base of it, an arm's length underground, is a metal crossbar, sunk into the cement. Attached to the crossbar is a set of handcuffs.

"This is a sleeping dragon," Nutmeg says. "Dragon for short. Basically, you lie on the plank, reach underground, and cuff yourself to the crossbar. Then you lock the fire door around your arm. The cuffs have a latch; you can open it with your hand if you want, but no one can cut you out of it against your will. It would take them days to dig you out. You can stay there for hours if you need to; the only thing that sucks is when your hand starts to swell."

Jeff eyes it, looking kind of scared of it and intrigued at the same time. I don't get why anyone would want to handcuff themselves for hours to a steel crossbar in a bucket sunk in concrete in the ground. "What's the point?" I ask.

"To block the road," Nutmeg answers.

I suddenly realize what they meant when they said the Free State's here to "stop the loggers." They meant literally. These people are here to lie down on the ground in front of moving trucks so they can't get in to cut the trees. I remember the face of the guy at the Quik-Mart, how he looked at us like someone who hurt his family. And I wonder: if that guy was the one behind the wheel, if he would stop.

I can hear the engine rumbling toward us, louder. Now it's close enough that I can tell it's a truck. "So who's locking down?" Sage says. "We gotta decide."

"I'd do it," Nutmeg says, "but I still have to finish the other dragons. No one knows how to do the foundations but me, and we can't really afford to lose a week if I go to jail."

"Right," Aaron says. "And there's a warrant out on Exile still from the Elk Creek action. And Sage and I need to handle logistics. Shit." Aaron's calm cracks and I can see his mind whir. "No one's here yet. It's too early." Sticks crack beneath the wheels of the truck as it gets closer. Dirtrat's faded to the edges of the group, almost blending into the forest.

I look at Jeff. Usually the chance to face down a corrupt authority figure would make his day. He'd probably quote some Crass lyrics, go in there ready for a fight, sure he'd win. But last night when he tried that with his dad, he lost. I remember the hurt in his eyes when his dad stared down at him, how skinny he looked in the face of his dad's shadow. How he realized he was losing. It did something to him. He looks down at the dirt. I can tell that he's embarrassed not to be the one he usually is, the one who's stepping up. And then I realize: maybe that's the thing that he could need from me. Maybe I can be the one to do it, and because I'm his girlfriend, it'll be like he did it, sort of, and he won't be embarrassed anymore.

"I'll do it," I say. And then I hear myself and panic. What the hell did I just volunteer for? But everybody looks at me, grateful. And now I have no choice.

CHAPTER 5

I can smell the dirt, moist and cool beneath me. My cheek is flat against the hard metal of the fire door, arm reaching underground into the dragon, the rest of me curled on my side on the soil. I can't remember ever lying on the bare ground before, without a sleeping bag or a tent or a towel. The cuffs circle my wrist in the dragon, hand clasped around the crossbar. I can see how your arm would fall asleep after a while, but for now it's all right.

Sage crouches down beside me, whispering fast as the engine gets closer. "Okay. So we don't know who's in that truck. Like I said: could be nobody, in which case they'll drive up, probably look at you weird, and leave. If it's Forest Service, you could be here longer." She hands me a bottle of water. "Don't drink too much so you don't get stuck having to pee." Crap. That hadn't occurred to me. "If it's really long—like overnight—someone'll eventually come in and relieve you."

Overnight? I hadn't thought of that when I volunteered. I hadn't actually thought of anything. I have to go home tonight. My mind starts racing, trying to find a way out of this, but the engine's getting louder. I imagine being out here in the dark, alone, chained to a weird random bucket in the ground, some forest cop trying to arrest me. I look to Jeff for help, but he's out on the fringes of the group, watching me with this weird mix of admiration and jealousy.

That's not how I thought he'd look at me when I said I'd do this. I thought I'd make him feel less alone, like he could keep going, like he does for me at home, that he'd realize he needs me like I need him. I thought he'd say thank you. But when I finally meet his eyes, he ping-pongs his gaze off mine, bounces it onto the ground.

Sage leans in closer to me, blond hair on her forearms glinting in the early-evening sun. "Listen," she says. "You'll be fine. We'll be watching from the woods, okay? Aaron and I will stay near enough that we can keep an eye on things. Nobody leaves anyone alone out here." My hair's in my face; I try to push it out of my eyes with my free hand, but it's clumsy and uncomfortable. Sage reaches down and does it for me. It almost makes me shy.

Usually I don't care what other girls think of me; I just expect them to be mean. But Sage isn't, and for some reason

I want her to think I'm strong. I clench my jaw, trying to cover up the fear underneath. "You're okay," she says. Jesus, she notices everything. "Just relax." Then she gets up and walks away.

Exile and Nutmeg fade back into the forest; Aaron says, "Thank you, Alison," and disappears. I look at Jeff. I want him to come sit with me, even though I know he can't. I want to say, *I'm scared,* but he's far away; I'd have to yell. I want to tell him, *I'm doing this for you.* But there's just this kind of awkward moment where we look at each other, and then he holds up his fist like some protester in a movie from history class and follows everyone else into the woods.

And then they're gone, and the engine's getting louder, and I'm lying here handcuffed to the frigging ground. Adrenaline courses through my veins. Even though I know I could unlock myself, I feel trapped. Like fall of sophomore year, when the senior jocks would swarm me in the halls, hitting on me in a pack; like that spring when girls pinned me up against a locker yelling, *Slut.* I know this feeling: fight-or-flight. But now I'm chained to the ground, and I can't do either one.

Wheels grind over dirt and then the truck comes around the bend. It's not the Forest Service. The truck is old and kind of rickety, paint chipping off in spots, an NRA sticker on the windshield, two-by-fours clattering in the back. The truck gets twenty feet away, then ten, and still it doesn't stop. I grit my teeth and hold my breath. Twigs fly in my face.

Finally it stops, like six feet from my nose. The ignition

shuts off and the doors swing open, and two guys get out. My heart beats so hard, it scares me; I wonder what a heart attack feels like.

For some reason I expected whoever was in there would be old enough to get me in trouble, but these guys aren't much older than anyone here besides me. One has stringy hair and a weaselly face; another one is chunky in the football-player way. They're wearing jean jackets, and both of them look mean. I hold my breath.

Weasel Face strides up from the driver's side and glares down at me. I can smell the beer, and suddenly I feel like I'm going to throw up.

"You gonna let us through, or what?" he sneers.

I don't know what to say, so I just say "No."

"What if we wanna get through anyway?"

I shrug, suddenly nostalgic for the jocks at school.

Football takes a step forward to stand with Weasel, threatening. "There's not enough room to drive around you."

"I know," I say. Then, brave or reckless: "That's kind of the point."

Weasel sneers down at me. "Y'know, no one out here likes hippies."

"Yeah," Football chimes in. "Y'all smell."

"I'm not a hippie," I tell them. I'm not positive I don't smell right now, so I don't defend myself on that charge.

"Yeah?" Weasel takes another step toward me, his work boot near my face. He bends to stare me down. I can smell the booze on his breath; I swallow back bile. "Then what're you doin' out here?"

My hand shakes, gripping the crossbar in the dragon. What do I say? *My boyfriend got kicked out and his weird punk friend brought us to the forest?* I strap on my bravado, pretending he's one of the jocks. "I don't know, what are you doing out here?"

"Came to give you a warning. You stop along the way up from the city, people see you. We know each other around here. Not like you." I realize: the guy at the Quik-Mart must've told them he saw us. And then I realize: that means it's not just that one guy who hates us—it's everyone who lives up here.

There's a long silence while they stare me down; my head goes light, my heart flutters high in my chest. Weasel's close enough to kick me in the face, and he's looking at me like he wants to. But I don't drop his gaze.

Finally he says, "Aw, fuck it," and turns to Football. "We don't need this shit." He starts to walk off, but then he turns to me again. "Go back to Seattle or Eugene or wherever you come from," he hisses. "We don't want you here." And then he spits. On me. I hold up my free hand to shield my face; it hits my sleeve, thick and stringy. As bad as it ever gets at school, I've never been spit on before. I rub my sleeve on the ground, cleaning it off with the dirt, as they get back into their truck and drive away.

For a minute it's silent, and I realize it's dark out. I didn't even notice that the sun went down. But now I can't see.

Then Sage and Aaron run out from the woods. "Fuck yeah!" Sage hollers.

"You okay?" Aaron asks as he comes to help me out of the dragon. He's close enough that I can see the protective look in his eye, and I feel this pang in my gut. No one's looked at me like that for a long time. It makes me blush and I want to look away, but there's no place to look; I'm chained to the ground.

"Yeah, I'm good." I lift my head and he unlatches the fire door and I snap myself out of the cuffs. Aaron gives me his elbow to lean on while I stand and I shake out my arm. It did fall asleep while I was there; I didn't even notice. I hold on to his arm a second too long, feeling the strength beneath his T-shirt sleeve. Standing up, I get a head rush. And then another rush: *I did this.*

Aaron and Sage's flashlights trace paths through the trees as we walk, lighting the dew on the moss. When we get back, there's a fire going, Nutmeg and Exile with a guitar, Jeff and Dirtrat beside them. Jeff's smoking a cigarette; Nutmeg gives him a coffee can. "For the butts," I hear him say. Seeing Jeff, I suddenly feel nervous: I was trying to help him when I locked down, but I don't think that's how he took it, and I don't know why, or how he's going to act with me.

Sage calls out, "Hey!" and everyone turns to look. "Look who I got!"

Jeff sees me, drops the coffee can, and runs up. He grabs onto me, his sinewy arms tight around my waist. "I'm glad you're okay," he says, and relief floods me like rain. I feel like I can breathe again. I pull back and look at him: that weird jealous look is gone. Now his eyes just say he's glad I'm back. That's the look I wanted. The one that says I'm not the only one who needs something.

"She did fuckin' awesome," Sage says, and I haven't had so many people be nice to me since I was a kid. I try to memorize the feeling. I don't know when I'll get it again.

I look at the huddle of people around me, the black sparking sky above the trees. Home feels a million miles away, even though it's only two and a half hours. And as soon as I think the word *home*, I realize: shit. It's late.

Too late to get back tonight.

I've never stayed out overnight, not without my mom knowing where I am. I don't even know what she'd do. Would she call the police? I don't have a curfew, but staying out all night is like an invisible line I've never crossed.

But then Jeff wraps his arm around my waist, claiming me, and I don't want that to stop. *It's not like she'll care,* I tell myself. *She's probably too depressed to even notice.* I don't believe myself, not quite, but Jeff leans into me and I breathe him in and think, *He needs me here. That's all that matters. Someone needs me.*

I wake up in a borrowed sleeping bag with Jeff, twigs creasing my face, dawn slivering the branches above me. It's Saturday;

the empty day stretches in front of me like a road. Birds ring in my ears, loud without a roof to muffle the sound, and I realize how much of the world our houses keep out.

Jeff breathes next to me, still sleeping. I bury my face in his shoulder, wrap my leg over his. With my eyes closed I can pretend it's just us out here, like in his basement on the tweedy couch, safe.

Then a loud burp comes from the other side of Jeff. Dirtrat's right there, curled up on a tattered yoga mat. Burping in his sleep. Lovely.

I sit up and rub my eyes and look around. Across the clearing, Sage and Nutmeg are sleeping in their tents; Exile's tent is open, his sleeping bag empty. Clinking sounds come from the kitchen, and when I look, I see Aaron there, pouring water into a big pot, then oatmeal from a jar. He waves me over. I look down at Jeff, wanting to stay with him, but I'm awake. Dirtrat burps again and that does it: I stretch as I stand up, grubby in my slept-in clothes.

In the kitchen Aaron sets me up with some almonds and a knife and I chop, enough for everyone. Exile brings coffee from the campfire; it tastes earthy and sharp in my mouth. As the sun brightens and the air warms, everyone stirs, one by one. Finally Jeff comes over wanting coffee. He slides his arm around me, kissing me hello on the mouth. He doesn't usually do that, kiss hello: too couple-y for him. It's nice. And then for a second I flash on my parents in our linoleum kitchen, in the morning before school, before my dad was gone, before everything. I flinch and pull away.

Jeff notices, and looks at me a second. I want to say, *No, it isn't you,* but I don't know how to explain. Then wheels turn in his head and he looks at Aaron. Jeff's hand leaves my waist; he takes a coffee mug and stares at Aaron again.

There's this awkward pause, like he wants to say something, but he doesn't, and somehow I feel like I'm supposed to decide what happens next.

That's not the way it is at home. At home he makes the plans and I ride in the passenger seat. I like it that way; he's always taking me somewhere, on adventures or at least away. I like how he chooses what he wants to do; I like watching him decide things. But now he's got this hesitation, the same one that happened when they were asking who would lock down in the dragon, this almost saying something but not saying it. I'm not used to that.

"You need anything else here?" I finally ask Aaron.

"Nah, I'm good," Aaron says, adjusting his stocking cap over his scraggly hair, smiling at me, then at Jeff. Jeff doesn't smile back. "You guys hang out."

I feel weirdly relieved.

I refill my coffee and lead us toward the fire pit. As soon as we get away from Aaron, Jeff's shoulders relax.

"Big move you made last night," he says as we sit. I guess we aren't going to finish our conversation about what happens when he stays and I have to go home. That's okay, though. That means I can pretend that it won't happen, at least for a little while.

"Yeah, I don't know, I just thought—y'know, nobody else could really do it." He looks hurt, and suddenly I realize how that sounded. "I mean," I scramble, "other people could've. But I don't know, for some reason I just said I would."

"Yeah." He nods, playing with his lip ring. Sometimes I see his face like it's new again and remember how cute he is. I'm still surprised a guy as hot as him is into me. "Did it hurt?"

"My arm fell asleep," I say, relaxing a little. "But it was weird, I didn't notice till it was over, I guess because of the adrenaline? Those guys were pretty intense."

"Yeah?" Jeff's eyes get almost mad. "What'd they say?"

"They called me a hippie," I say, and laugh.

He laughs back, and I'm relieved. "That's fuckin' hilarious."

"I know, right?"

"So, was it like . . ." he trails off, looking for words. "I don't know. Was it cool?" He looks at me: I can tell he's really asking.

"Yeah, it was," I say. "I mean, it was super-scary, too; they'd drunk so much, I could smell it coming off them. One of them spit on me."

"They spit on you? What the fuck?" He stabs a stick into the dirt. "I can't believe they did that!" He looks weirdly guilty. Like he should've kept that from happening to me. I want to tell him that it's okay that I was the one to do it, that how everybody acted afterward gave me something to be proud of. But then I think, that would sound like he doesn't have anything to be proud of. So I don't say anything.

All day long we don't talk about going home, even when the sun starts to set and the light through the trees gets dappled and dim. Jeff and I eat together, pretending everything is normal, and Aaron shows me how to build a fire and Nutmeg shows me how to pour concrete, and my hair smells like campfire and my hands feel strong. Somewhere in my head I tell myself that if I just don't do anything, don't make a choice to stay or go, I can just stay here with Jeff and keep pretending Tacoma doesn't exist, and maybe it'll turn into the truth.

Jeff and I sleep curled up together again, three nights in a row now, and it starts to feel like just the way things are. It's not till the sun arcs to the center of the sky and starts its slow climb down that I start to get antsy. Today is Sunday. That means tomorrow is Monday. And first period is chem lab. I've ignored it as long as I can, but then finally I can't.

I find Jeff, alone, whittling a stick into a point with a Swiss Army knife, and kick his boot. "Hey." I plop down next to him. "So."

"So," he says back.

"Tomorrow's Monday."

"Yeah?" he says, like, *So what?*

"I've got school?"

"Okay," he says. "What, you want to go or something?" He grins, trying to turn it into a joke.

"No." I grin back. I can't help it; his charm is contagious. "But if I'm not at lab tomorrow, I don't graduate. Remember? That's why you waited for me Friday morning?"

His face falls. I guess he's been trying not to think about it, too. "Shit," he says.

"Yeah," I say.

"What are you gonna do?"

"Well, I mean, I have to go back." I pick at a pebble.

"Really?" His voice softens, disappointed. He knows I hate it at home. He knows I hate school. After everything that happened this weekend, he must've been hoping I'd just throw it all away. But I can hear Andy in my head: *C'mon, Al. Don't be a dumb-ass.* And I think about that letter tucked behind my mirror, the one from Antioch. It's stupid, but something won't let me let it go.

Jeff and I don't really talk about college. I mean, he knows about my mom and UCSB and Andy's scholarship, but all I've told him is that it's bullshit, that I don't want to go. He says I could come down to Portland after graduation and live with him and his band in the house that they're getting, and usually I nod and act like that's what'll probably happen. I can't tell him about Antioch; he'd think it was so stupid. College is the Man; you go there and you're buying into the system; dropping out of Evergreen was the best decision he's ever made. I can hear exactly what he'd say: *There's no way you can even go; who'd pay for it? Besides, what's it gonna do, funnel you into some sellout job you don't even want? It's stupid. Forget about that, come live with me and my band, at least we're doing something.*

"I mean, do you have to go back?" he says. "'Cause you could just—"

I don't let him finish. "Yeah."

"You remember I can't go back to my house, right?" he says then, like, *You know what you're deciding?*

I nod. I know. He just looks at me; we just look at each other. And this huge space opens up between us. We have to be in different places. He can't go back, not now, and I can't stay. I wish I knew how long he'll have to be here, that we could figure out some kind of plan. I feel like I might cry. I haven't cried in front of another person since the last time I tried to talk to my mom about Andy.

"Do you want to go back?" he asks me, tentative.

"No," I tell him. "I just have to."

He raises his eyebrows, doubting, like, *Okay, if you say so.* Like he thinks I have a choice. I don't know how to explain to him that there's no choice. He doesn't know that I can still hear what Andy's voice sounds like in my head. He doesn't know that hearing disappointment in that voice is worse than hearing disappointment in anybody else's. He doesn't know that it's my fault Andy's gone, and that the least I can do is not let down the memory of him. I don't know how to explain that. So I just sit there, feeling far away.

"Okay," he finally says. The forest is silent around us.

"So can you drive me back?"

"Yeah, all right." He digs at the dirt with a stick. "We have to leave before it gets dark, though."

"Right."

"And then I'll head back here in the morning, I guess."

My heart sinks. "Yeah," I say. "Okay." I know there's no way it could happen, he doesn't even have a place to live, but: I wish he'd bring me back and stay. I wish he needed me enough to make him just say, *Fuck it, I'll figure it out,* and stay with me in Tacoma, to pick me up and take me out and help me escape all the things I can't get away from on my own.

CHAPTER 6

Sage and Aaron hug me goodbye next to Grandpa. Sage pulls back, her hands on my shoulders, freckles framing her hazel eyes. "Sucks you're going," she says, and I look at the ground, guilty. "Glad we got you while we did, though," she turns it around. Jeff reminds them like three times that he'll be back soon. I guess he's not thinking about how it might feel for me to hear him say that.

We bump over the dirt road, past the tarps and the hand-painted signs, retracing our steps. Gradually the dirt turns to asphalt, county roads, and I watch out the window as trailers start to dot the forest, ramshackle houses with moss-spotted roofs. They're ugly, but there are few enough that they blend in with the woods instead of taking over. As we drive, the buildings multiply, three in a row and then four, convenience store gas station diner. I try to skip over them, keep my gaze on the beautiful parts, branches curving black against sky, green patches silvered with rain; I try to hold on to it as long as I can.

When we merge onto the highway, the woods slip away, giving way to McDonald's and Walmart and malls, concrete monstrosities, and suddenly they look like monsters to me, Godzilla stomping out the screaming world beneath his feet. It all just looked like the normal world before, but all of a sudden the plastic and gloss and too-bright colors remind me of Naomi and her lipstick, the jock guys in their polyester jerseys. I remember the dirt in the forest, soft beneath my cheek; I realize that's what's under all these strip malls, smothered by fake brightness, and for some reason I almost start to cry.

Jeff hears me clearing my throat and looks at me sideways. I try to look down so he won't see, but he does. "What's wrong?" he says, and I don't know how to explain it, so I just say, "Nothing."

"Are you crying?" he says, his eyes on me, drifting too close to the car in the next lane.

I don't answer.

"Are you?" he says again. I don't cry in front of people; I don't know what he'd do if I told him yes.

"No," I say. "Whatever."

He drifts again, his eyes on me; the car beside us honks. I have to give him something. "I'm just not psyched to go deal with my mom."

"Yeah," he says. "That sucks." He thinks a minute.

"Least you've got a place to live, though, right?" *Unlike me.*

"Yeah," I say, staring out the window, wishing I could rip those fucking ugly strip malls off their foundations and expose the real world underneath.

Once we're back into the city, the buildings pile up on each other so quickly that it's hard to remember there's anything else, and ugly just turns back into normal. We stop at the diner and I get us dinner and then coffee and then a bunch of refills, trying to delay the inevitable as long as possible. Finally Jeff says, "So I can crash with you, right?" and I realize I hadn't even thought of that. My chest fills up: I'm so relieved, thinking of spending the night with him. I don't even care that I might get in trouble. I just don't want him to go.

"Sure," I say. "I'll sneak you in. Let's just wait till she's asleep."

I twist the doorknob slow so it doesn't creak, and Jeff takes off his boots outside. I shut the door silent behind us and wait. Nothing. I was gone the entire weekend, and she's just sleeping. She's not up, waiting, wondering where I am. My heart sinks a little, but I don't know what I thought would be different. She doesn't need me.

We slip into my room and into the bed, cocooned beneath the comforter. Jeff doesn't try anything, and for once I'm relieved; I'm already feeling way too much. I'm feeling the dirt floor of the forest beneath my cheek, the rub and scrape of it, all those people saying *thank you*. My world's been so small since Andy died: trying to keep my head down, get through, keep everyone but Jeff away. I'm not used to people seeing me. I want to hide, and bolt; to huddle up and run away. Jeff lies behind me, close, his arm slung over my waist, and I nestle backward into him, trying to pretend he'll be here past tonight. If Jeff weren't here, the black hole of my house would swallow up this whole past weekend, suck it down and down till it turned into a tiny dot and disappeared. But Jeff was there with me, somewhere outside of this; that makes it real. I repeat it in my head—*it was real, it was real, it was real*—until I fall asleep.

The beep of my alarm jolts me awake, and for a second I'm confused, until I look around and realize where I am. My heart sinks. Right. Here. My life. Jeff snores through the alarm; I decide to let him sleep a little longer. I switch off the alarm, click my door shut quietly, and go to take a shower.

On the way to the bathroom I crack the door to Andy's room. It's like a museum, the old house of some dead president, gussied up for tourists: everything exactly in the place where it was when a person lived here. It's the only part of our house my mom ever cleans. The living room, the kitchen, the den: they all get gross and messy, full of dust. But Andy's room is spotless. I look at the Pearl Jam posters hanging next to Zeppelin, his T-shirts folded, camping gear stacked perfect in the corner. No one wants it this way but her. It doesn't keep him alive; it just makes the memory of him hover here, circling around the remnants of what his life used to look like. I grab Andy's tent and sleeping bag on the way out of his room, just to spite her. Maybe Jeff can use it.

The shower feels amazing after three days in the woods; hot water blazes clean trails through the dirt on my skin. I'm a little sad to wash the campfire smell out of my hair; I say a silent goodbye as it swirls down the drain and the water runs clean.

I'm walking back to my room when I hear a thunk above me.

Shit.

I clutch the towel around me with one hand, grip Andy's tent with the other, and rush into my room. Jeff's awake; he's getting dressed. I'm naked, though. "She's up," I hiss-whisper, pulling underwear and jeans on, fast. Then I hear her on the stairs.

"Alison?"

"Hi," I holler, fingers fumbling to hook my bra. Jeff is gesturing frantically at me, some weird kind of desperate sign language, asking what he should do. It feels like something from a movie, except I don't have space beneath my bed or a window he can climb through.

And then the door to my room opens, no knock, and she walks in and finds me in my bra and Jeff fully dressed and my bed unmade, and it's obvious that he slept here. Her eyes go wide; rage rushes in to fill them like a flood. "Alison." Her voice is thick with accusation.

I steel myself, muscles turning to armor as I turn away to put a shirt on.

Jeff keeps his head down like a beta dog, picks up his pack, and tries to leave my room, but my mom blocks his way. "I'm sorry," he mutters.

"Don't talk to me," she tells him, still blocking his path. She's skinnier than him, but she's not moving. She turns to me. "Alison," she says.

I stand there, frozen, hot, skin prickly like a rash. "*Alison,*" she says again, but then nothing else. Like it's a heavy bag she set on the ground, and she's expecting me to pick it up for her.

"What?" I finally ask. I'm not giving her more than that.

She looks at me, stunned that I'm not scrambling to explain myself. "What the hell do you mean, what? Where were you?"

I'm not giving her one speck of where I was. Not a stone or leaf or piece of dirt. Not a name, not a town, not a road—nothing that would let her take what's mine and make a picture of it in her head. There's one thing that I realized I can do this weekend: I can refuse. I can lie down in the middle of the road and I can lock myself up and I can refuse to move. I've done it once before. So now I try it on her.

"Nowhere," I say. In my peripheral vision I see Jeff look at me, shocked.

"Nowhere? Alison, you were gone for two days!"

Locked in, clamped down. "So what."

"So what?" her voice climbs upward.

"Yeah, so what," I say, adrenaline kicking in. I've never done this before: just flat-out defied her. Never in my life. I've always shut my mouth, kept my head down, given her just enough to keep her off my back. I've never even imagined I could say, *This is what I'm doing, whether you like it or not.* I'm dizzy from it, like at the top of the hill on the roller coaster just before you dip down and your stomach is suspended midair. "I went out. Get over it."

She looks at me, shocked, and digs in. "I'm not going to 'get over it,' Alison! You're grounded. For a month. At *least*. No, you know what? Two months." She looks at me like she won and now I'm supposed to give up and go hide in the corner.

"And what if I don't listen to you?"

"You don't have a choice." She takes a step toward me. Her cheeks are red, her eyes awake now. I feel Jeff behind me; he takes a step toward me, too. He has my back.

"Sure I do," I say. "I'm not grounded. I'm going out. See? Easy as that."

She takes another step. "I am your mother, Alison." I can feel her breath: it's too much, too close, too crowded.

"No, you're not." I shove her off me, hard. The heat in my chest floods my arms down into my fingers.

She stumbles backward; I just keep going. I'm hurtling downhill too fast to stop now, even if I wanted to. "Were you my mom when you locked yourself up in your fucking room and cried for two fucking years? How about when you let Dad leave? Fuck you. You haven't been my mom since Andy died." Telling the truth is a good kind of pain, like when I jam a safety pin through my earlobe and the blood comes out, hot and sharp, striking through the thick dull of everything else.

She steps back like I hit her. "What're you so shocked about?" I say. "It's true. All you care about is what you've been through and everything you've lost. You don't give a shit about me. So quit trying to pretend you do." Now I'm up in her face, and her eyes are welling up. "You just want me to be what Andy was so you can feel like he never died. But he did, okay? He died. But I'm alive. And you don't get to say what I do and what I don't. Not anymore. I'm not going to fucking UCSB, and I'm not fucking staying here."

Her eyes panic and she scrambles. "You can't do that, Alison. You can't—"

"You can't fix it," I cut her off. "And I can't fix it either. Andy died. Our family broke. And you've been using me to try to put it back together, but it doesn't work that way. It doesn't work." I'm crying now, for real, tears hot on my cheeks, and I don't care. "It doesn't work," I yell, from a place way down past where I can control. "I'm done fixing it for you." And then I lie: "I'm moving out. Okay? I'm moving in with Jeff. And there's nothing you can do to stop me." And then I grab

Jeff, who grabs our stuff, and we run out, letting the door slam shut behind us.

I pound the wet pavement toward Jeff's car, yank the door open, and jump in. He throws our stuff in the backseat.

"Are you okay—?" he starts to ask, but I cut him off.

"Drive," I tell him, my rib cage heaving hard. He fumbles for the keys.

"Drive," I say again. He does. Once we're in motion, he looks over at me, checking on me. I don't want to talk yet.

I roll down the window, letting the damp wind cool my burning cheeks, and slowly I stop sweating and catch my breath. "I'm not going to school," I finally say. "Don't take me there."

He looks at me confused. "Wait. You're not going to class? Does that mean . . ."

"I don't know. No."

"But you said if you missed lab, you don't—"

"Just stop fucking questioning me, okay?" I snap. I can't think about that right now. Not at all.

He pauses for a second.

"Sorry," I say, still a little rough.

He tries again. "So are you saying—?"

"Yes," I say. Then I take a breath and settle. "Yes, that's what I'm saying." It feels weird in my mouth, sounds weirder in my ears. I think of Andy again, and my chest crumples with shame. Like I'm killing something inside me.

But I can't go back and live with her again. I can't. Not after that.

"Okay," he says, then a second later, "Are you sure?" He takes his eyes off the road to look at me, and someone honks.

I don't think it even matters if I'm sure. I think I made the choice already. The stuff I told my mom—that's the kind of thing you can't come back from. "Yes," I tell him, yes, I'm sure I want to be with you and I want to leave this place and school is miserable and I'm sick of trying to be something I'm not for someone else when I don't even know what I want to be for my own self, and the Free State is weird and it's illegal but at least people saw me there, for what I am, not a reputation or a tragedy, not a story or a symbol, not the legacy of someone else's life or its hope for resurrection, just Alison, just me.

I wrap my hand around his on the gearshift. "Yes, I'm sure."

And then he guns the engine and we drive away from my whole entire life.

CHAPTER 7

When we get back to the Free State, it's already gotten bigger. There's an old school bus parked in the clearing, chalky black primer painted over the yellow. I stand on tiptoe to see in the scuffed-up windows and all the seats are gone, replaced with a plywood loft and a cookstove, milk crates holding filmy baggies of dried beans and rice. The brown mini-fridge is covered with punk-band stickers; dirty T-shirts litter the floor.

"Alison!" I turn, caught snooping. Sage runs toward me, T-shirt sleeves pushed up to show her strong shoulders and tattoos. "I didn't think you'd come back!" She throws her arms around me; it makes me shy, but I let her.

"Hey." Jeff tilts his chin at her, like *I'm here too.*

She looks at him a second, then says "Hey" back.

"So what's the deal with the—" I jump in, pointing at the bus.

"Oh! Yeah," Sage says. "I guess word got out about your lockdown."

"Wow," Jeff says. He looks at me.

"Yeah," Sage says, not pulling her gaze off me. "People in Portland heard shit was going down, so a bus came up for support. They stopped in Eugene and picked up some guys on the way."

"That's crazy. How'd they even know?" I'm not used to people doing things because of anything I do.

"When people hear things are heating up, they come around. Want to make sure we've got support. And then some people, y'know, they like it. Wanna get in the fight." Sage eyes Jeff. "Your friend's over by the kitchen," she tells him, meaning Dirtrat.

Jeff looks at me like I'm supposed to come with him, but Sage looks at me like I'm not. I feel caught for a second; I want to go with Jeff, but I don't want to have to choose. Finally I tell Jeff, "I'll catch up with you later, okay?" He looks a little stung, and I want to say, *I'm sorry, wait, I'll come,* but he heads off too fast.

Later Nutmeg brings me to the front lines to help him with the dragons. The buckets of wet cement are heavy and I want to just let him do it, but he says, "Here," and props up the bottom so I can pour the sludge into the hole he's dug. Plastic cuts my fingers; it takes my whole body's strength to keep the bucket up and aimed right. But he helps me, and I do it, and before it dries, we sink a crossbar in, wedging the metal into the sticky, thick cement, lining it up so it'll stay steady even when someone's trying to take it apart.

"You built stuff before?" he says after we've built two more.

I shake my head.

"Natural talent, I guess." He grins, and I realize: it's the first time in years anyone has told me I was good at anything. The knot in my chest loosens a little. Maybe if he saw this, Andy wouldn't think I was an idiot for leaving school. Maybe he'd see that I'm good at something, too. Maybe it would be okay with him. I tell myself, *I'm doing something; it's okay with him,* over and over, till a tiny part of me starts to believe it.

We walk back toward the fire pit and the kitchen, sweat drying sticky on my cheeks. The new kids are there, five of them with Aaron and Exile, eating some kind of tofu glop with spaghetti sauce. They heard about us from some campus action group, although I'm not sure they actually go to college. The guys all have a lot of tattoos like Jeff and Dirtrat; there's one girl with purple hair and a lip ring who scares me immediately. The other girl is super-skinny; her blond head is shaved, except for, like, this fringe of bangs, her T-shirt is dirty, and she never looks at anyone except for one of the guys—Bender, I hear someone call him. I'm pretty sure he's her boyfriend.

I'm finishing my glop when Jeff and Dirtrat come from

the direction of the car. Dirtrat scrapes the dregs from the tofu pot and plops down on the ground. Jeff sits next to me, close enough to touch, and I lean into him, feeling his flat stomach beneath my spine, following his breath. I look around and realize that right now, I have something I haven't had in a long time: people who want to be around me, who aren't mean or trying to get something from me. I haven't had that since I was in the van with Andy and his friends. I feel like a normal person for the first time in a long time.

Later on I lie in Andy's tent with Jeff, looking out the mesh window at the sky. I set it up when it was still light out, just to see it. I remember it from when we were kids, the green tent with its orange cords. Andy showed me how to put it together way back then; today I was surprised I still remembered. I drove the stakes into the ground, clicked the poles together, saying to him in my head, *See, I'm still doing what you showed me. I'm still listening to you.* My sleeping bag is laid out inside it and I can feel the rocks through it, poking through the softness. I curl into Jeff and listen to his steady breath, sleeping.

As Jeff's breathing slows down, I stare out at the huge sky, and my mind speeds up. And I realize: I just left my life today. My heart races as the thought sinks in, this high-up anxiety in my ribs that feels like it'll speed faster and faster till my heartbeat spins out and I can't keep up. I threw everything away. My mom, my school, my house. I hate it all, but it's all I had, and I can't believe it's gone. Everything is gone. Well, except for Jeff. I still have that. I grab onto that, clench it tight in my mind, repeat it over and over, *I'm here with him,* until my heart slows down and I can breathe. I breathe in his smell, trying to swallow it, keep it inside me, keep him inside me, something solid to hang on to.

The next morning when I wake up, he's already gone. I rub my eyes, pick the dirt from my fingernails, and emerge from the tent, blinking back sunlight. I hear him before I see him, over by the school bus with the punk kids and Dirtrat. The guys are talking shit, punching each other on the arms, joking, loud. They remind me of John McDonnell and the guys at school, except with piercings. They have a ringleader, too, this guy with a black patched-up jacket, louder than the rest. The guys jockey for position around him, try to top each other while he listens. Purple-hair girl is like one of the guys except beautiful—loud and elbowy, taking up space. The baldhead girl—I heard someone call her Naya—just sits there, sleepy, laughing at their jokes. Crass blares from tinny speakers inside the bus, interrupting the birds. Jeff laughs again and I stand there, watching. He doesn't see me.

For some reason I feel uneasy, rudderless. The same feeling as in the tent last night, but worse now, because he's over there. Not here with me. "Shut the fuck up, Bender!"

the black-jacket guy yells at Naya's boyfriend. The purple-haired girl calls him a capitalist pig. Jeff laughs, another joke that I don't get. I look away.

Aaron's in the kitchen, doing dishes. As he dries the last one, he looks up and catches me watching him. I blush.

Shit.

But he just smiles. He looks over to Jeff at the bus, then me, and puts his dish towel down and walks over to me.

When he gets to where I'm standing, he says, "Hey—are those shoes comfortable?"

I look down at my Docs, spattered with mud, ten times more worn than they were a week ago. "Yeah? I guess."

"Good. Come for a hike with me?"

I look at him, his worn tan Carhartts, his crinkly eyes that know things, older, certain. He wants me to come with him? If I was blushing before, now my face must be like a fucking cherry.

I look back to Jeff at the bus, the guys around him; I smell pot smoke. Naya digs in her backpack like she's looking for something, then disappears inside the bus. Another guy swigs from a flask. Dirtrat laughs at something. Jeff still doesn't see me.

I feel guilty, but I want to go.

"Okay."

CHAPTER 8

We hike past the kitchen, out of the camp, till the woods thicken and the clearing ends. I look for a trail, but all I see are ferns. I hang back, not knowing where to walk; Aaron senses it and turns around. "Just follow me," he says, reading my mind.

In a few minutes we're out of earshot, and I suddenly get nervous. The trail is narrow; brambles scratch my arms through the sleeves of my flannel. I don't know him. We're alone, just me and him, and I don't know why he brought me here, or if I should have come. Maybe I didn't try hard enough to get Jeff's attention; maybe I should have checked with him. I remember that look on his face when Sage wanted me to hang out with her, when Nutmeg asked me to help him with the dragons. Maybe I shouldn't be here.

My nerves build up and mix with creeping guilt and it

adds up, piling onto itself, until I finally blurt, "I came here to the Free State with Jeff, y'know."

The seconds after that open like a chasm.

It's possible that I might be the biggest asshole that ever lived.

I hear his footsteps on the leaves; my face is hot.

He finally says, "I know."

I am the biggest asshole that ever lived.

"Sorry," I mumble. "I didn't mean I thought—"

He stops and turns around. His eyes are kind. "I know," he says again. "It's okay." I squint at him, trying to see what he's hiding, but his eyes are too clear to be lying. There's nothing to uncover. "Sage is my girlfriend."

"Okay," I say. "Sorry."

"No worries."

We walk in silence for a while; that rudderless feeling just gets worse as we go deeper into the woods.

After a long time, Aaron says, "So." I jump a little, startled. Branches interlace above us, pale green lichen dripping off black silhouettes, sunlight filtering through the canopy. "You just came up here 'cause your boyfriend did, right?"

I look at him, embarrassed. It's true, but somehow I feel like I should have a better reason. "I guess so? I mean, there were a few things."

He just waits.

"I mean, he got kicked out of his house, and I got in a fight with my mom."

"Right," Aaron says.

My heart thunks. I can't tell what he's thinking, and for some reason I care.

"But your first night here—that was pretty cool what you did." He lets it hang there, like it's a question.

"Thanks?" I say, not sure that's the right answer.

"Sure, yeah," he says, like that wasn't the point. "But I mean, where did that come from?"

"Me locking down?" I ask. He nods. I don't really want to tell him the reason: that I could tell Jeff thought that he was supposed to be the one, and I didn't want him to feel bad he wasn't doing it. But I also feel like Aaron is a person you don't lie to. "I guess—it felt like nobody else really could, so I sort of had to."

He nods. "But you didn't have to."

It's like he's arguing with me, sort of, except he's being kind. It's weird, and I can't find my footing. "Okay?"

"I mean, it's still a decision to stand up when nobody else can. That says something about you." I guess I must look insecure, because he smiles at me and says, "Something good, I mean."

"Oh." I feel relieved, even though I'm still not exactly sure what he's talking about.

"So I thought I'd show you something," he says. The forest has thickened as we've walked deeper in; moss blankets the tree trunks like green velvet. "Since you've got that in you. I thought you should see the reason that we're up here."

"Okay," I say.

What I really want to say is *Why?* Why is he bringing me out here and not Dirtrat, or Jeff, or any of the school-bus kids. What does he mean, *You've got that in you?* But I don't want things to be weird, and I don't want him to think I think that I'm special or something.

"Some of these trees are five, six hundred years old," he says. "The framework for a whole system that's been here that long—animals, all the other plants. Once you cut them, you can't get that back. And there's one really special one back here; she's more than a thousand years old. We call her Legacy."

I mean, a thousand-year-old tree, that's cool, but I don't get why he's bringing me all this way to see it. It also seems pretty weird that they would give it a name, and call it "her." It's not a person.

The trail narrows even more; branches reach up and over our heads to make a tunnel that holds us. It's like pictures of fairyland in children's books, except it's real. We walk and walk, and he doesn't talk anymore, and eventually that stops making me uncomfortable and I get used to the silence, and then suddenly the path ends and the woods open up, and I see what he means.

I've been in forests during Andy's Scout trips; I've whizzed by a million trees on highways; I've camped out here. But this is different, and suddenly I understand why he brought me all this way.

Pretend you're standing on a sidewalk, looking at a skyscraper a thousand times taller than a person, so tall you can't even see the top of it as it narrows to a point and merges with the sky. Pretend you're dwarfed by it: your hands, your bones, your life suddenly tinier than dollhouse miniatures, smaller than specks on the ground out the window of an airplane, minuscule dots in the shadow of this huge thing before you.

Now imagine that this thing wasn't built by hands the size of yours, wasn't put together by a person out of steel and stone and glass, but is actually *alive*, like you are, covered in green moss and lichen, glistening with raindrops and crawling with creatures, squirrels ducking in and out of its trunk, whole colonies of ants, entire worlds coexisting, fitting together perfectly on the body of this one ancient thing. And looking at it, just looking at a stupid *tree*, you somehow understand what math is, what biology is, and chemistry: it's all a map of *this*, this perfect equation where every part fits perfectly into the whole, and the whole is part of larger wholes, and these are part of even others, and out and out and up and up, past what your mind can picture, every part of it alive. And you suddenly understand, in a way you haven't ever realized, that you are alive, that you're a part of it. You're not like asphalt and Kmart; houses, Doritos, and cars. You're like this. And for a minute, just a minute, the ground is solid underneath your feet, and you feel safe.

CHAPTER 9

We hike back in silence, not wanting to erase what we just saw. It's weird that it could give me all those feelings. It seems silly that it's this big intense thing: I mean, it's a tree. A bigger version of all the trees around us. But somehow the scale of it turned it into something else. It was bigger than a building, older than a person; it made being small feel like a good thing. I haven't felt that since I was little. Even if it's stupid, I try to hang on to that feeling. I want that back.

When we get back to the fire pit, the sun is setting. Left-over light slivers through tree-branch silhouettes, making patterns like lace on the ground, and I see the math of it, here, too, how everything fits together, intricate and inter-connected. And then I look up and see Jeff. I see him see me, and then Aaron, Jeff's eyes measuring the space between us. I see the math of that, too.

When Aaron wades into the group to help make dinner,

Jeff sidles up beside me. "Where'd you go?" I can't look at him; I don't know if he'll be mad.

I want to explain what happened, seeing Legacy, but I'm not sure it'd make sense to him. "We just went on a hike."

"You were gone a while." I still don't want to look at him. "What were you guys doing?"

"Nothing," I say, and he just looks at me. "I mean, it's not like that." I hope it's dark enough that he can't see my cheeks flush. "Sage is his girlfriend."

"Uh-huh," he says, suspicious. "Then how come you guys were gone so long?"

He's never been jealous before. I feel guilty, but I also feel this kind of satisfaction, knowing he needs me, that those guys by the school bus aren't more important to him. For a minute I look at his eyes above his sharp cheekbones and it occurs to me I have some power, that I could rub it in if I wanted.

But I back away from that. I don't want to hurt him. "He just wanted to show me Legacy," I tell him. "The really big tree? The one we're protecting."

"Yeah, but why'd he only take you?"

He only took me because I was the one who locked down. Because he saw something special about me then. But I can't tell Jeff that. So I just look at him.

"I mean, did you ask him to?" he asks.

"I mean, it just sort of happened—"

"How?"

"Well, he invited me out there—"

"Right," he says. "But why just you?"

This conversation is starting to make me feel far away from him, and shitty. Like I did something wrong, even though I didn't. "I'm not really sure," I say, and tell the truth, because now I kind of have to. "I think it had something to do with me locking down that night? I think he wanted to show me because of that. Like to show me what we're fighting for."

As soon as it's out of my mouth, I know it was the exact wrong thing to say. He's looking at me with that same weird mix of admiration and jealousy as the night that I locked down—but now it isn't jealousy of Aaron, it's jealousy of *me*.

I backtrack: "Look, I came back here to be with you. Okay? I'm here with you. Not someone else. Don't worry about Aaron. It wasn't like that."

He looks at me.

"I'm here with you." I need him to believe me. He's still the only thing I have. I look right into his eyes.

His gaze flickers and he looks down. "Yeah," he says. "Okay."

After dinner I help Sage and Aaron with the dishes, water washing the grit from my fingernails. Exile starts the campfire, and the flames snake upward as the sun sinks behind the trees, day turning to dark. Halfway through rinsing I look up and see Jeff head over to Dirtrat and those school-bus kids. The loud one with the black patched-up jacket is apparently named Stone; he seems meaner than the rest, with squinty eyes. I can tell by the way everyone clusters around him that he's the boss. Jeff offers him a cigarette, which is crazy; he's got one pack of American Spirits with him. I'm shocked he'd share. Stone takes it, motions for Jeff to sit with all of them, and pulls out a flask.

I squint through the smoke to watch them; they're too far away to hear, but I see Jeff lean in, impressed. It reminds me of how Jeff looked at me that first day at Point Defiance Park, like I was as smart as him, like I was someone that he'd want to know.

The next morning the sunlight pries my eyelids open and I watch Jeff sleep beside me. Last night, falling asleep, I kept thinking about my hike with Aaron. How he saw me, picked me out; how being near that tree I saw the math and patterns and aliveness that were all one thing; how safe and small and holy that made me feel for those ten minutes, and how that feeling seemed totally normal for Aaron. That means he's had that feeling before. Lots of times. That means he knows all kinds of things I want to know.

Aaron saw something in me, though I have no idea what, and in the woods he showed me things and assumed I'd understand them. I wanted to know more about those things. I wanted someone who could show me all of them.

I don't know if Jeff can, I think to myself, watching him sleep. And then I flinch, because that thought scares the hell out of me. He's all I have. It's not like I'll ever wind up with

Aaron. Even if Aaron thought of me that way, which he doesn't, his girlfriend is the only female human on the planet who's basically ever been nice to me. I don't want to wreck that. I don't want to wreck whatever they have together. I don't want to wreck anything. I already did that. I wrecked my whole family. That's enough for an entire life.

I need to be with Jeff. But I also felt something out in the forest that I've never felt before, something better, and bigger, and real. I don't want to give that feeling up.

That means I need to make Jeff understand it.

Today I'm awake first, so I can stop him before he heads over to the bus with Stone and Goat and them. I can show him what I saw. I rustle his shoulder and wake him up. He grunts, then rolls over and rubs his eyes to look at me. "What's up?" he says, bleary.

"I want to show you something," I say, the same way Aaron said it to me.

After coffee we start on the path. Jeff starts to go first, but then realizes he doesn't know where we're going, and there's this awkward moment, like when you get stuck facing someone in the hallway and nobody's sure who's supposed to move first. Finally he takes a step back and I go in front of him. "Do you have, like, a map or something?"

"No." I shake my head. "I just remember where things are."

"Oh," he says like he's not sure what to do with that.

He falls in step behind me and it's weird not talking; I'm used to him always having something to say, and I don't know how to fill the space. I don't want to, really: I want that silence back from yesterday. But I don't know if it's okay with him.

We go up a hill and down it, and when we spill out onto flat, I can see the clearing up ahead, the one that's right near Legacy. I hear a rustling and look closer. There's movement.

"Shh." I stop him, nervous. I don't know if it's a person or what. Whoever it is, I don't think they should know we're here.

"What?" Jeff says, too loud.

"I saw something up there," I stage-whisper. "Shh."

I go ten steps ahead of him, creep up quietly toward the clearing. When I get there, sun dapples the branches, yellow and white; flecks of dust swirl in the air. I get close enough to see that it's a deer. She's eating, head bent to the grass, elegant and graceful. And behind her is Legacy, reaching clear into the sky.

I don't trust Jeff not to scare away the deer. I've never seen him really be careful with anything. But I have that feeling again, the one from yesterday. The feeling of something beautiful. I need him to know what that feels like.

I tiptoe back to get him. "C'mere," I whisper, as soft as I can manage. "Just be quiet, and go slow."

Shockingly, he does what I say. He walks closer, quieter than I've ever seen him, and when he gets near enough to spot the deer, he stops.

Then he sees Legacy. I watch him look up the trunk, all the way into the sky. I can't read his face. If he thinks it's stupid, or *it's just a tree*, that will mean he doesn't understand me. That I can't have the feeling I have out here and still be with him. That I have to be with someone else. But there isn't anybody else, not anybody I can have. My heart pounds. I wish I could make him feel how I need him to feel.

"Hey," he finally says, after a long, long time. "Thanks for leaving school and coming back with me. I know you didn't have to."

"Yeah," I say. "Thanks for bringing me," and for a minute I realize: maybe this is that thing I felt the day we met in Point Defiance Park. That he could take me somewhere else, away from my life and someplace better. Someplace more real. Maybe this is that. Some small voice in my head says, *But you're the one who brought him out here to the tree*, but I push that down, and then he pulls me in to him, and I lay my head on his chest, his hoodie zipper cool against my cheek, and we stay like that a long time.

CHAPTER 10

The next week I spend my days working hard, hauling and building and carrying, my muscles used up and aching by each night. It helps keep my mind off my mom, the sound of the front door slamming behind me, the last time I'll ever hear that sound. I do things I've never done: lug water, cook food, build fires. I've never really *worked* before, not with my body, not like this. I've done homework and made people coffee, and that's not the same. This is something we can hold in our hands, that feeds us, warms us, keeps us safe. Like Andy and his Scout troop, everyone working together to get through the woods. I'm good at it. When I get tired, I remind myself, *This is what you wanted. You wanted something real,* and I believe it.

We're all supposed to work; the agreement is that the whole camp comes to meetings every morning and we divvy up chores for the day—building barricades, cooking, dishes, firewood. The reality is more like: Sage, Aaron, Nutmeg, Exile, and me do stuff, and the other people smoke pot and talk about being radical a lot. Aaron says it's better to "lead by example, not coercion," and I kind of see what he means: I certainly don't want to be the one telling guys with face tattoos to help with the dishes.

I do wish Jeff were with me working, though. He's mostly with those bus kids now, especially Stone and Goat; it's like they're his people, like he's got a pack. He always talked about his band that way, too, and I remember being jealous of that feeling: like you had people who you knew were yours. Like you belonged. I like the work here, cooking for people and building with my hands, but I want to be with Jeff. I wish I didn't have to choose.

One night I'm on cleanup duty after dinner, scrubbing a rice pot, steel wool scraping under my fingernails, when Jeff comes over. "Just let it soak," he says. "Come hang out on the bus."

I look at Aaron and Sage, both stacking up supplies, then over to the bus. Sage catches me.

"It's okay," she hollers over. "I got it. It'll be easier after it soaks a while anyway." I feel kind of bad, like I'm flaking on them. I need to earn my right to be here, the food I eat. My mom never stopped reminding me of that: how hard she worked, how much she sacrificed for me. I don't want to be a freeloader.

Jeff looks at me. "C'mon," he says. "Live a little," and he smiles. Like a punk show in Seattle, a late-night drive with the windows rolled down. Like there's some adventure he's not afraid to have. It's always been my favorite thing about him.

"Okay," I say, and we head to the bus as the sun sets.

Inside is pretty awesome, I have to admit. It's a school bus, like the kind I rode in elementary school, driver's seat up front and the black ridged rubber aisle down the middle, but the seats are all ripped out, and in their place are these skinny wooden bunks built into the walls. Below each bunk is a row of milk crates, dirty clothes stuffed in with old half-shredded issues of *The Stranger*, typewritten Xeroxed zines, dog-eared books with titles like *No Gods No Masters* and *Pussycat Riot*. In the back by the emergency exit there's even a little kitchen: a sink with plastic tubing and a mini-fridge, dirty dishes and spilling bags of rice. It's a lot grosser than the one at camp, but it's still cool to see that someone built a kitchen in a bus.

We turn the corner off the stairs, standing by the vinyl driver's seat. Naya and her boyfriend, Bender, are lying in the farthest bunk, back by the kitchen. I think they're sleeping when I first see them, and look to Jeff—maybe we should go? But Jeff says, "Hey," and Naya lifts her head.

"Hey," she says thinly. "'Sup."

"Where is everyone?" he asks, and Naya chuckles. I'm pretty sure her boyfriend is actually asleep.

"Probably off starting fires or some shit," she says and then lies back down, cuddling into her boyfriend.

It's awkward for a second and I look at Jeff again like *We should go?* but then the emergency door clatters open and the other guys tumble in from outside.

"What's up!" Stone says, loud, and I guess it doesn't matter to him that anyone's trying to sleep. Jeff smiles when he sees him, and the guys come up and clamber on the bunks near us. Stone sits and starts rolling a cigarette, muddy boots on the sheets. Dirtrat sits beside him, watching over his shoulder, and Stone chucks his arm. "You're not getting any."

Goat sits on the bunk across from them, and Jeff plops down beside him. There's not really enough room for me on the mattress, too, so I just stand there.

"Where's Cyn?" Jeff asks Stone.

"Ah, her hair was fading, so she went down to the stream to dye it again."

Not that I'm a biologist or anything, but it seems weird to me that you'd put a bunch of purple hair dye in a stream if you're out here protecting the forest. It can't be good for the fish. I must make a face, because Stone goes, "What?"

"I mean. Isn't that kinda not ecological?"

He laughs and does the bicep smack of universal brotherhood on Dirtrat. Stone's strong, I think; Dirtrat kind of recoils. "Ha!"

I just look at him.

"You're kidding, right?"

"She's kidding," Jeff says. I fucking hate that shit.

"Not really." I shoot Jeff a look. "It's purple hair dye."

"Okay, hippie police," Stone says.

I just stare at him. I'm not the police.

"Chill, Alison, it's vegetable dye," Stone says.

"That shit is vegan." Dirtrat laughs, shoveling stale tortilla chips into his mouth.

I look at Jeff. He's laughing along with them. I don't want to be the lame girlfriend. And anyway, maybe he's right. What am I, the hippie police? The fish will probably be fine. "Whatever," I say, and crack a grin. "Fuck the fish."

Jeff pulls me down onto his lap. The sheets smell like unwashed body now that I'm down here, but I'm glad to be close to him. He wraps his skinny arms around my waist, claiming me, and it helps me feel like I belong.

An hour later it's dark and all the guys are drunk. Crass is blaring from a tinny-speakered boom box, and astoundingly Naya and Bender have continued to sleep through it all. Cyn still isn't back from dying her hair, which is fine with me. We've never even talked, but the way she looks at me makes me feel like Naomi Gladstone and her posse do, her cheekbones sharp, that mean-girl harshness pointing from her eyes. I'm glad to stay away from her.

Stone, Goat, Jeff, and Dirtrat are embroiled in a noisy debate about property destruction versus violence, and whether there's a tactical difference between monkey-wrenching an engine and punching a logger in the face. Personally I haven't seen any of them do either one, and I don't know about these other guys, but Jeff and Dirtrat didn't have the balls to even stick around that first night, much less punch someone. But whatever. I think they all just like to use the word *tactical*. Every once in a while I'll jump in with a snide remark. If I stay mostly quiet, my timing is good, little sister mostly listening, sometimes serving up a zinger. I know how to do that in a group of guys; I make them laugh. I didn't realize I'd remember how to do that.

Goat and Dirtrat are laughing at some dumb thing I said, and Jeff's looking at me, proud. I look around the lightbulb-lit bus and I think, *This is pretty okay.* The music on the boom box is hard-core punk, not Zeppelin, and it stinks a little more, but it kind of reminds me of the van. I relax back into Jeff, leaning on him, and close my eyes. The throng of guy voices around me blur into a haze of rowdy laughter, and it doesn't matter what they're saying, just that they're here and I'm included and I have someone to lean on, someone looking out for me. For a minute I let myself feel young again, like the girl before things happened, before I knew the things I know. I reach for her, that kid, the one who felt safe, who wasn't by herself. The one who was on the inside, not outside alone. I can almost reach her.

Then, "Alison," Stone yells, jolting me out of my reverie. I open my eyes. He's holding out the plastic bottle of Popov vodka—"the brand of bums," Jeff calls it—pushing it too close to my face. "You dind't have any," he slurs.

"I'm good," I say, the sharp smell coming off his skin, cutting through the thick of male stink.

"Aw, c'mon. It's capitalist not to share," he says, and I

mean, I could see what he means if it were my booze, but I don't quite see the political problem with not taking his.

"Yeah, I'm not a capitalist," I say. "I just don't drink." Jeff is arguing with Goat and Dirtrat about some shit about British skinheads in the eighties. His arm's not on me anymore.

"Come on," Stone says. "Help you loosen up."

He holds my eyes too long, the way Brandon did in the van the first time, after Andy died; I recognize that look. It means *I want something from you.* I hate that look.

"I'm loose enough," I say, trying to fend him off, and the second I hear the words come out of my mouth, I regret them. Shit.

He smiles. "Y'are, huh?" He looks at Jeff. "She is?"

Jeff's halfway through a sentence about the ideology of some band called The Oppressed; he's not really listening. "Sure," he tells Stone. "Whatever." Then he turns to Goat and says, "See, that's what you get when you let people in who aren't on board for the mission, man—"

Stone looks at me too long again. Jeff's not paying attention. "So you don't think you need to loosen up," Stone says. "I think you do," and now he reminds me of John McDonnell in the hallways, that up-and-down that wants something and hates you at the same time, and Jeff is laughing with the other guys and doesn't even notice, even when I take his hand and put it on me, saying, *Claim me, make him stop.* Naya's snoring in the back bunk and there's no other girls in here, just a tangle of testosterone and sweat, the loud male laughter that an hour ago felt safe, felt almost like a home I used to know, but now with the vodka and the smoke and the too-grown-up-ness feels like the exact opposite: like that home going away, like it turning dangerous. The walls feel too close and the bunks feel too narrow and the smoke is clogging my eyes and Stone is still staring, waiting, challenging me to come up with a comeback that I know he'll turn against me.

He blinks and I blink, and I can't think of anything brave to say. He grins at me, winning, and I finally can't stand it. I stand up and touch Jeff on the shoulder. He's talking and he doesn't turn around. I lean down and say in his ear, "Hey, I'm going to bed," and he turns halfway back and goes, "Cool, cool," and goes back to whatever he was saying.

I just hang there for a second. It's fucked up to me that Jeff's all weird about Aaron, who doesn't want a thing from me, who's actually my friend, and yet he doesn't even notice when his drunk buddy hits on me. It makes me feel like maybe Jeff's whole jealousy thing isn't even about me. Like it's more about guys and how they are with each other. Aaron's the leader of the whole group here; Stone's the leader of the bus. But Aaron doesn't even want to be a leader; he's just powerful. He doesn't believe in climbing that whole ladder, he believes in something else. Something about people doing things together, not who's on top and who's beneath. Whenever Jeff tries to climb up to where he thinks Aaron is, Aaron just looks at him like, *Why are you climbing. Just come be on the ground with us and work.* But Stone is on the ladder. The same one that John McDonnell's on, the one that Jeff and Dirtrat understand, the pyramid of guys jockeying for position, trying to get closest to the guy at the top. Stone says something to Goat, and Jeff laughs the loudest; Stone hands the bottle of Popov to him and Jeff drinks, looking like he feels safe, looking at home. It's not about me. It's about guys and who they are to each other. My body just happens to be between them. I slip out the school-bus doors and no one even notices.

When I step out, the air opens back up. The walls dissolve and the thick stink of the bus dissipates into fresh air. The forest breathes around me; I feel safe. Everyone else is sleeping already, the camp put away, the embers burned out. I make my way to our tent and nestle down in Andy's sleeping bag, the nylon smooth against my cheek, the twigs pressing up beneath my body. I'm alone here, but it's better than being in that bus. I can hear their voices echo through the woods, far away but still loud against the silence of the forest, and I wish they would shut up, and I wish Jeff would leave that bus and come back into the quiet with me.

After that, Jeff starts staying on the bus till late every night. I don't go back there with him; I don't want to. During the day, there's always stuff to do, so Stone and them don't bother me: they can help if they want, or they can talk about stupid punk bands and the revolution, it doesn't really matter. I keep focused on my work, the calluses growing on my hands, the muscles in my legs, and I don't let Stone get close to me again.

At school I could never figure out how to do that, keep people away if I didn't want to talk to them: we were all together in the halls, you had to be in certain places certain times, there was no escape. But here there aren't those rules, there's just work to do, and I get to decide what I do and when, how I contribute, and who I want to see. It makes me feel strong. Like I get to choose who I'm with, but I don't have to hide from anyone.

I miss Jeff in the tent at night, though. I never ask him to come back early; it would just annoy him. I go to bed when the work is done, when the fire is out, when the forest quiets down and everyone else in the tents turns in. I fall asleep alone as the drunk voices echo far away in the bus, and he always comes back eventually. When he unzips the tent door, I stir, open up my arms to him, and he rustles in with me. I pretend to be sleeping so we won't have to talk, and we hang on to each other till dawn.

For those few hours every night I focus on the things that are still the same. I hold on tight and drink him in, trying to match our edges up again. He falls asleep while I lie there, waiting for sleep to take me back again. I listen to the voices start to slow down on the bus and try not to think about all the things that I can't talk about: the tug in my gut when I remember my mom, the anxiety about dropping out of school, the creeping nerves of knowing I'm going to have to do something after all of this, the knot of dark guilt about Andy, the feeling Aaron might know things that could set me free from all of that.

CHAPTER 11

One morning Jeff's still sleeping in our tent and I've been up since dawn, watching the light go from navy to pink to golden through the trees, making a huge vat of gluey oatmeal. I had to scrape it together from a few different tubs, and there's no maple syrup or honey or anything left to add to it. Local hippies have been bringing food up here since we came: castoffs from the food co-op, bulk rice and wilted broccoli. But this week no one could come, and there are a lot of us now. We're running out of food.

Aaron comes to the kitchen as the pot is bubbling, another early riser. "Hey," he says, and I smile at him: "Morning."

"I've gotta make a food run," he says. "I could use an extra set of hands; Sage is helping Nutmeg with the barricades today. You up for it?"

I hesitate. The whole weirdness with Jeff started when I went hiking with Aaron. And that was basically right here, near us, in the woods. A food run would mean driving off the premises, away from the forest, back into the world. Together.

But then: "C'mon." Aaron smiles. "It'll be fun." And his green eyes crinkle, kind, and my heartbeat speeds up, and I say, "Okay." As we walk away from the clearing, I see Jeff come out from our tent, rubbing his eyes. I don't turn to find out if he sees me leaving, but I think he does.

The car is rickety and super-old, like from 1985 or something. The tape player doesn't work. It's weird to see Aaron driving; I've only ever seen him in the woods. He grips the wheel in his tan Carhartts and navy hoodie, a burgundy stocking cap over his head. In the car, away from the forest, he looks like a normal person, just regular like everyone else.

We bump over dirt roads and the rocks in them until finally we get to the paved parts. I'm embarrassed to find myself relieved at the ease of the asphalt, a hint of civilization smoothing things out, softening the ride. The last time I made this drive the asphalt almost made me cry, but now it's nice for things to feel easy for a second. My shoulders drop and I start thinking about gas station bathrooms and sinks with running water and I'm glad I came on the supply run.

It's half an hour to the tiny timber town. We drive on county roads, no strip malls or highways. It goes slow.

"So, Tacoma, huh?" he says after a while. "You miss it ever?"

"No," I snort, looking out the window. "Not at all."

"You have people there, or . . . ?" He lets it hang.

I don't want to lie, and I kind of have to answer, even though I don't want to. "My mom."

Aaron thinks a second, then turns and looks at me. "How old are you?"

"Um . . . seventeen?" I don't know why I feel weird telling him that, but I do.

"You're not eighteen," he says. I shake my head. "That's good to know." Then, carefully, "Does your mom know you're here?"

"No," I tell him quickly, suddenly worried he might say I have to go home. "She thinks Jeff and I are in Portland with his band." And then, not really a lie but not exactly the truth, "She let me go."

"Ah," he says. "Okay."

"She doesn't miss me," I say, bravado steadying my voice like in the hallways at school.

He takes his eyes off the road for a second. His voice softens. "Are you sure?"

I don't tell him about the secret tiny grain of hope buried so deep I can hardly even feel it anymore. "Yeah, I'm pretty sure," I say. But my voice cracks.

"What's that about, Al?" he asks. *Al.* A nickname. My chest hitches. He looks at me again; I turn my head toward the window so he won't see the wet in my eyes.

"She's got other . . . stuff she's thinking about," I say, still not looking at him.

He just waits.

"A few years ago . . ." I trail off, realizing I'm about to tell him about Andy. My heart starts beating really fast; I've never really talked to anyone about it. Not all of it. I mean, Jeff knows he died; he knows what happened afterward. But he doesn't know that it's my fault. Nobody does. Somehow I know that if I open up the door to Aaron right now, I'll tell him everything.

"A few years ago what?"

I watch the road: nothing but trees and trees and trees and a few scattered houses with mossy walls and waterlogged roofs. I listen to the whir of the engine. We drive over bumps in the road. I shift my weight.

Finally: "A few years ago my mom started drinking."

"Oh," he says.

"Yeah," I say. I feel like he can tell there's more.

"That must be hard," he says. "I'm sorry."

I can feel the knot of tears in my throat, threatening to burst out. I swallow hard. "Yeah," I tell him. "Thanks."

Closer to town, rusty trailers start cropping up, brown and beige dotting the stretches of green, kids' toys and old cars cluttering front lawns. People squint at our car windows, trying to see inside. Our bumper stickers say "Walk in Balance" and "Support Organic Farmers." I brace myself, remembering the Quik-Mart, that guy who thought we wanted to take away his job.

Aaron knows the way to the little health food store, tucked into a strip between a pawnshop and a check-cashing place. We park the car and get out. Next to the shops is someone's house; a boy and a girl play on a faded pink plastic slide out front. She looks about four; he's probably seven. "Hi," the girl blurts as we walk by, shy and curious. "Hi." I smile back, and her mom glares at me from the porch. For a second I think about my own mom, how once she must've sat like that with us, but then I push it away.

In the health food store, I head straight for the bathroom. I don't even have to go; I just want the running water.

I turn the hot water up as high as I can stand, even though I know it's wasteful, and I let it run over my hands and wrists. I wash my face with liquid soap, dry it with paper towels, and I know they're dead trees but it feels so good to get really clean. Not camping clean from a stream or water jug; civilization clean, from a faucet and soap. In the mirror I can see the line between my face and neck; the rest of me is two shades darker, grubby and tan, like somebody who works the docks, or in someone's yard. My cheeks are pink and naked. I haven't looked in a mirror in two weeks: my eyes look older, skin freckled and rough. I wonder if I would look different to people from school, if they'd be able to tell that I've changed.

I walk out, awake and scrubbed, and find Aaron in the aisles. It's weird to be in a store. And it's even weirder that it feels so strange to be there. There are price tags; fluorescent light bounces off the linoleum floor. Lonely boxes of organic macaroni dot the metal shelves, and they look sad to me, these products, strange and unnatural. It's amazing how fast things can start looking unfamiliar.

The store is tiny, almost empty; it doesn't take long to get through the aisles. Aaron puts things into the cart: rice and lentils from the bulk section, canisters of oats. A hippie-looking lady works the register; it's hard to tell how old she is because she looks so tired. She checks out our clothes as she's ringing us up and says, "You guys from that Free State, huh?"

It makes me nervous that she's asking: so far everyone in this town seems to hate us, and I don't know if she's one of us or one of them. I've never thought about the world like that before, but now I have to. I'm part of a thing that's defined against another thing, opposed and opposite. It makes me feel scared of the world and safer in it at the same time. I guess I picked sides.

I look to Aaron: I don't know whether we're supposed to keep it secret. He looks into her eyes, direct and steady, and says, "Why do you ask?"

She says, "I think what they're doing up there is brave."

"Well, thanks," Aaron says, answering her question without answering it. "I think we all just pretty much feel like we have to. Just doing what we can."

The lady nods and leans in. "Cascade really wants that sale to go through, you know."

"Well, yeah," Aaron chuckles. "Timber companies tend to want to cut the trees they think are theirs."

"Sure." The lady nods. "But they think it sets some kind of precedent if they let this one get stopped."

I don't really know what that means, but Aaron nods, sober. "That's good to know," he says, thinking hard. "Thank you."

"Sure," hippie lady says, surprised at his seriousness. "That'll be $78.39." Aaron doesn't say anything else, so I don't either. He takes cash from his pocket and pays her while I load the food into cardboard boxes.

I help him haul the food back to Exile's car. My arms have gotten strong. Aaron is quiet while we get the food into the trunk, but as soon as we're in the car with the doors closed, he says, "It's good we went there."

"Yeah." I'm not sure exactly what he means. "How come?"

"It's important information. That Cascade sees this as symbolic." He starts the car. "That means they're probably planning to dig in. And that means we should too."

CHAPTER 12

When we pull up to camp, it's already past lunch-time. I'm unloading the car, Aaron hauling boxes to the kitchen, and Jeff comes out from the school bus, purple-hair Cyn behind him. She looks at me, pretty in her hard way, and I wonder where the other guys are, if it was just them in there. He waves her off—*just a minute*—as he beelines toward me, jaw set.

"Where were you?" he asks as he gets closer, and it's not like when he'd call me forgetting I was at school, it's like when his dad kicked him out and he yelled at me. His voice is sharp. My shoulders go tense.

"On a food run?" I tell him. I see Aaron clock us from the kitchen, keeping his eyes on us as he unpacks lentils and rice.

"With Aaron, right?" It's like an accusation.

There aren't a ton of people around, but we're not alone. My cheeks go hot.

"Yes, with Aaron, so?"

He just laughs, this angry kind of snort. "Fuckin' A," he says, snide. "Of course."

"Of course what?" I ask. I mean, I know *of course what*. Jeff knows me. He can probably feel something. But I haven't let anything show, and I won't. Sage would hate me, Aaron would get weird, and it would totally mess up me and Jeff—though suddenly, the way he's talking to me now, that last part seems way less important. "What are you even talking about?"

"You know what? Fuck you, Alison," Jeff says.

I look at him, shocked.

A week and a half ago we were out at Legacy together; he said *thank you*. I don't understand how he got from that to this.

I freeze, not knowing how to fix it. From the corner of my eye I see Aaron put the food down.

"Hey," Aaron hollers over. "Hey, Jeff," and that makes it worse. Jeff's eyes are blazing like that night with his dad, and I don't know what he's going to say next. Suddenly I don't trust him; I can't predict what he's going to do. It feels like he's going to fight. I don't want him to fight. Not here. Not Aaron. I feel like I have to say something, but I don't know what.

Aaron walks over toward us, wiping his hands on a rag; Jeff squares his shoulders. I hold my breath.

But when Aaron gets to us, he's calm. "Hey, man," he tells

Jeff. "It looks like things might heat up here in the next week or so; I heard some stuff in town. I could really use your help."

That throws Jeff. I see him on his heels, wheels turning, trying to figure out what Aaron's doing. He thought Aaron was about to be an asshole, but now he's asking for his help. "What kind of help?" He's skeptical. I'm just glad to have his attention off me for a minute so I can breathe.

"Sounds like Cascade Lumber's gearing up, so we need to make sure the entry points are fortified. Sage and Nutmeg are finishing the dragons, but we need some ditches behind them. Like monster potholes, deep enough to snare a tire or break a shock absorber. I need someone strong to get that done."

Jeff's lip twitches a little when Aaron calls him *strong*. I can tell he wants to take the compliment, but he doesn't trust it. He eyes Aaron, sussing him out. "Yeah?"

"Yeah. You think you could do that? Would really help the camp."

Jeff looks to me. I don't want to say the wrong thing, so I don't say anything.

"Yeah, okay," he finally says. "I guess I can help out."

"Awesome," Aaron says. "Thank you so much. That's huge. Exile will set you up with gear—probably take you a few hours today and most of tomorrow. Feel free to hit some of those guys up to help you out"—he gestures toward the school bus—"but you lead it. Cool?"

You lead.

I see Jeff take that in, and I see Aaron make sure he does.

Jeff looks at me like he's thinking something, but then he just says, "See you later, Alison," and walks off.

That night when Jeff huddles up beside me in the sleeping bag, I just lie there. He was asleep already when I came into the tent, worn out from a day of digging. I'm awake, watching the moonlight glow through the mesh. His skinny chest presses against my shoulder blades and I squirm beneath the weight of his tattooed arm, trying to stake out enough space to breathe.

I'm pissed at him. He yelled at me today. And I don't know if anyone but Aaron heard it, but the point is, Jeff didn't care if they did. He's always made such a big deal that I embarrass him when I don't know random punk shit, but he apparently doesn't give a shit about embarrassing me in front of everyone here.

I feel guilty that his feelings are hurt, but I also know I didn't do anything wrong. It makes me mad that I feel guilty, because I know I shouldn't. It's like the guilt and the mad are in a knot I can't untangle, and it just makes me want to get away from him.

And it's not even like he's got a better reason than me to be jealous. I didn't say anything to him about stupid purple-haired Cyn behind him in that school bus, or ask what they were doing when me and Aaron were in town.

I left my life to come and be with him. Even if I hate my life, that should count for something. But I guess it doesn't.

CHAPTER 13

When I wake up, Jeff's already gone. I'm relieved I haven't had to talk to him since he yelled at me yesterday; I don't know what I would say. But then I lie there in the half dawn, watching the sky turn pink through the mesh, and I start worrying. I really don't have anyone else here. I mean, Aaron's my friend, and Sage is nice to me, but I just met them. It's not like I've ever tested things with them, like I really know that I could lean on them. Who says they even care about me. Maybe they're just being friendly. I start thinking about my mom, her shocked face when I left, the raw red anger right before that. I think about what I told Aaron in the car yesterday, that she doesn't miss me. That's what I tell myself. I'm pretty sure it's true; if it isn't, it's still what I'd rather believe.

I hide in the tent as camp starts to clink awake. My mind is racing, from thing to thing to thing: Jeff, my mom, what the hell I'm even doing here, what I'll do when I finally have to leave. I guess I convinced myself that what I told my mom might actually be true, that I could follow Jeff to Portland after this, but now I'm not sure I can do that anymore.

That acceptance letter from Antioch is still folded in my backpack, crushed at the bottom, edges softened with backpack lint. I can't go. There's no money, and my mom would never help me even if she could. But ever since it showed up in our mailbox, I haven't been able to throw it out. It's like it's taunting me, something that I want and can't have. I don't even know why I care. It's not like I've ever been there, like I know anything besides that stupid guidance counselor's catalog. It's not like I even believe in college. But I keep thinking about it.

Jeff, my mom, and my future circle through my brain like a hamster wheel, fast and faster. It speeds up till I can't lie still anymore, and I sit up and I'm awake. I need to know what's going on with Jeff. We can't avoid each other here. I pour some bottled water on my hand and wipe the dirt off my face and head out of the tent.

I hike through the woods, listening for voices. I'm pretty sure Jeff wouldn't bring Stone—Aaron said *you lead*, and I saw Jeff's face. I know he wants the chance to prove he can. But I hope he doesn't have Dirtrat there, or Goat or *them*. And I definitely hope that he didn't take Cyn.

When I get to the front lines, I'm relieved to see there's no one from the school bus there. Probably he tried, but they're all still passed out.

When I get close, he says "Hey," but nothing else. He just keeps digging. I consider asking if he's still mad, what's going on, but something tells me to wait.

There's a spare shovel on the ground. I pick it up, start working next to him, silent. Having something to do takes the edge off.

For a long time he just digs beside me, spindly in his tattered black hoodie, tattoos poking out from his rolled-up sleeves. I can't tell if he's tired or mad or thinks everything is fine. I wish I could read his mind: I want to know what's in it, but I don't want to ask.

Finally he frowns at me, and then at the ditch I'm digging. "That's not deep enough, Alison," he says. "A truck with good tires can drive right over it."

I don't say anything, but I think, *Asshole*.

"Whatever. I'm just saying," he says. I look at his ditch: it is deeper. Ugh. He's right. I start going back over mine, grinding my shovel into gravel.

He watches me a minute, and then, "Here," he says, and comes to help me out. I breathe in, relaxing a little. We work side by side, sweaty, and for a minute it feels like maybe he's going to try to make it better.

Then he opens his mouth.

"So, that was fucked up yesterday."

What I want to say is *Yeah, and it was your fault*. What I actually say is "You mean me going into town with Aaron?"

"Yeah, I mean, without telling me."

I don't know why I'm supposed to tell him where I'm going. Is that suddenly the rule? But I don't say that. Instead I just say, "I don't know."

"What do you mean, you don't know?" Sweat streams down his face.

"I mean, I don't know."

"Yeah, no," he says. "That's not how it works. You either agree with me or you don't. It's fucked up or it's not."

"I guess," I say.

"See, same thing," he says. "'*I guess.*' That doesn't mean anything." He sounds like he's making fun of me. I just look at him. He keeps talking. "At least take a stand, say what you think for once. Do you think it's fucked up that you didn't tell me where you were going, or do you not?"

I want to throw it back at him, ask him, *Do you think it's fucked up you were in that bus with Cyn, or do you not?* But I know that saying that would just make it worse. I don't want to just do what he's doing back at him. That always only makes the fight get bigger.

"Seriously, Alison," he says. "You better fucking answer me."

You better? What the fuck? He's never talked to me like that. He's never been this way with me: confrontational, angry. I've seen it aimed in a million other directions: his dad, the Man, the capitalist-industrial complex. But not at me. His eyes are blazing. It makes me feel like I can't reach him, like I'm not sure he recognizes me. I feel frozen, and I don't know what to say to make it stop.

"See?" he snorts. "You can't even answer. It's like I don't even know where I stand with you. Or why you're even here, or anything."

"Seriously?" I stare at him. "You don't know why I'm here." How does he think I got up here in the first place? *I'm here because he is.*

"Yeah, seriously. I mean, I don't have anywhere else to go. This is, like, a life decision for me. But you can have your little vacation and go hiking with Aaron and have your adventure and then just go back home—"

"Are you kidding me?" I say. I'm shocked. "Go back home? Did you hear the fight I got in with my mom?"

"Did she kick you out?"

"I mean, no, but—"

"Right, you left. So that means you can go back."

"Jeff, I dropped out of school—"

"So get your GED," he says. "And then you can go to college where Mommy got you a scholarship, and live in the dorms and go to football games and fuck frat boys or whatever the fuck—"

"Jeff, what are you even talking about—"

"Some of us don't have a choice, okay? I have to be here. I'm here. I don't have somewhere else to go."

"You're being crazy. I don't want to go home, with my

fucking stupid mom, and you know I don't want to go to UCSB—"

"Sure, right now you don't, but what happens when it gets uncomfortable? What happens when it gets hard? Or you get sick of being dirty, and not having any money, and living in the woods, or . . ." He trails off and looks away before he says what I'm pretty sure he's thinking, which is: *when you get sick of me.*

I just stare at him.

"I don't know," I finally say.

"See, that's the thing. That's what I'm talking about. You're either with me, or you're not. You're either out here for the long haul, or you're not. It's not like there's some gray area."

Jeff doesn't believe in gray areas. He never has. Things are right, or they're wrong. People are assholes, or they're not. That used to feel so safe to me: like the world was a place that I could manage, like there were answers and it was possible to know them. Now I'm not so sure.

"You're not answering me," he says. "You're not saying what you think. You're just fucking standing there," and he's right. I feel paralyzed. I flash back to rain beating on the asphalt driveway, that feeling that I couldn't say anything. That whatever I said wouldn't do any good.

"Jesus, Alison. Just take a fucking stand." The mad in his voice cracks just enough for me to hear the hurt beneath. "What do you want?" I think maybe he means *who.*

"What do you want?" he says again. "For real."

The quiet swells between us; I hear twigs crack in the distance.

What I feel is gray area, but I don't know how to say that. He won't understand.

Then, from where I heard the twigs crack, I hear Sage's voice.

"Alison!" she calls. "Hey! You got a sec?"

Jeff and I lock eyes. He knows he's not getting an answer, not now.

But the question isn't going away.

"Go ahead," he says, and takes the shovel from me. "I don't need your help. Just go."

Sage leads me farther down the road. Since we got back from town, she and Aaron are suddenly doing a lot more things: handing out tasks, putting people to work. Nutmeg's building barricades; Exile's rigging up a tripod down the mountain—three PVC pipes hitched together, with a platform, that someone locks in with a bike lock on their neck. She's even got some of the school-bus kids doing little stuff when they're out and around—but not anything important, nothing she and Aaron need to count on.

Now she needs my help stockpiling wood.

We walk down the road, closer to the main roadways. "You can go where you want, you know," she says as our feet crunch the gravel. "You don't need his permission." I guess she heard him tell me, *Go ahead. Just go.*

"I know," I say, embarrassed. I don't want her to think I'm weak. Even though I think I am.

She walks over to the gear pile and picks up two axes. "I'm not sure when we'll be able to go into town for firewood again, so we gotta do it ourselves." I hear the same tone that was in Aaron's voice when he said, *Cascade is planning to dig in; we should too.* "Anyhow this way we can use wood that's already fallen. In town we buy cut logs, which is kind of ironic, considering that's what we're trying to stop."

"Right," I say, but it makes me think. I mean, we build a fire every day, because we need to cook. Everybody has to cook. Most people have jobs: they don't have time to pick up branches off the ground and cut them up. They don't get their heat from a fire; they have to pay for electricity, from a power plant. That can't make them bad.

It makes me wonder what Sage and Aaron really think about people, whether they're judging everyone; it makes me wonder, if I were out there, whether they'd judge me. By the side of the road there's a clearing, a big stack of branches piled up. "So—if we couldn't cut our own wood, do you think it's wrong to buy it?" I ask Sage.

"Pretty much the root of the problem, huh?" Her eyes crinkle when she smiles. "Here, set this on that stump there," she says, handing me a log. And then: "I don't know the answer."

That freaks me out. Someone's supposed to know the answer. What are they all fighting so hard for if they're not

even sure? "But I mean, then—what are you guys doing here?"

"Well, I know what the answer isn't," she says. "I know it's not just to burn through everything and cut it down, which is what we're doing." She tapes up her hands.

"But like—people have to have jobs, and live in houses, and stuff."

"Yeah?" she says, like, *Go on*.

I think of my parents when I was just born and Andy was little. "People can't just all come and, like, live in the woods. Our food comes from stores, right? And we need to buy stuff, and have electricity and gas for cars." I think of the cashier at the health food store Aaron and I were just at, the fluorescent lights that lit the space, the plastic bags the rice came in. "That can't be all, just, bad."

She looks at me for a minute, taking me in. She looks sort of weirdly proud of me or something. I can't quite decode her face. "It's not," she says.

I feel relieved hearing her say that. Jeff and his friends are always all "*Fuck civilization!*" but I'm pretty sure I like civilization, mostly. And those guys certainly haven't presented any viable alternatives.

"And you're right," she goes on, "it's a privilege, in a way, to be out here. None of us has kids we have to feed, right, or a sick grandma whose rent we have to work a job to pay. We're all healthy; we've got tents, and warm-enough clothes. That's not true for everyone."

"So what's everyone else supposed to do, then?" I ask. I don't ask what's really in my head, which is *What are we even doing here?* I don't want her to be insulted. But that is what I'm thinking: what good is it to do all this, if there's only, like, twenty of us out here and everyone else still has to do all the same stuff back in the world? There's a lot more world out there than there is up here.

"I'm not sure, exactly," she says. "But I think we could figure it out if we would slow down and try. Humans are pretty amazing—we've figured out a lot of stuff before. If we can, like, put airplanes in the sky, and invent computers, I feel like we should be able to figure out how to live without destroying the planet, right?"

"I guess." She has a point, but she still hasn't said anything about *how*.

"But the first thing is, we have to admit we're destroying the planet. Which is kinda scary, you know. Most people don't want to think about that. Because of everything you're saying—like, *What else are we supposed to do?* So that's one reason I'm out here—to try to get people to think about it. If we can get people to pay attention, maybe more people will start to care. But also I'm just here to keep them from cutting shit and burning it down, where I can, like at least this one forest, this one place. Just to slow the whole thing down."

"But aren't you trying to stop the whole thing? It's still destroying the planet even if they do it slower, right?"

"Sure, but like you said, there's a lot of big things we'd need to structure differently. We can't just stop everything without having any alternatives. So I figure if we can slow them down, we can buy enough time to figure out a different way."

I try to picture my mom or my teachers sitting down and "figuring out" how to have electricity in a way that doesn't cut down forests. It seems ridiculous. "Do you really think that would happen?" I ask.

"I mean, we're figuring it out, right?" she says. "Like you and me, right here."

That terrifies me, suddenly, that idea. That all we have is what we figure out ourselves. I feel cut loose, unprotected, in a way I never have before. I guess I always just assumed someone was looking out for everything, protecting us, making sure the world ran right.

But what Sage is saying makes me realize that that isn't true. Nobody is just up there taking care of things. It's up to us. That scares the shit out of me.

"Here," she says. "Hold out your hands," and I do. She tapes them up like she did hers, and hands me an ax.

She puts the log on a stump. Then, "Watch," she says, and brings her ax down on the log swift and hard, splitting it. The noise is like a gunshot, loud enough to make me jump. She wipes her brow. "Okay, now you."

She sets down another log, then gets behind me and wraps her arms around me, positioning my hands on the handle. Her palms are calloused, her muscles strong; I feel spindly and girlish next to her. She steps away. "Okay, raise it over your shoulder, and—GO!"

The ax swings down and sinks halfway through. "Good," she says. "One more and you'll have it."

I'm lifting the ax again when I hear tires on the dirt road, over near the dragons. "Shit," I say. "You hear that?"

Sage stops for a second. Wheels crunch on gravel. "Yeah."

She doesn't have to tell me what to do. I drop my ax next to hers and we haul ass.

CHAPTER 14

From fifty feet away I can see the sirens on the truck. Cops. *Shit,* I think. *Shit shit shit. They're gonna fucking send me home.* And then I remember: Jeff was digging farther down from the dragons. They would have had to get past him to get here. My stomach sinks. We run.

When we get closer, I see Nutmeg's already locked down. Two guys in uniforms are looking down at him. My heart thuds hard in my chest; I crane my neck to see if they've got Jeff.

"Hang back," Sage whispers, her hand on my shoulder.

"But Jeff was down the road," I whisper back.

"If they've got him, there's nothing you can do right now. And Nutmeg's already there. Just go slow and let's watch."

All of a sudden my feet on the twigs are loud as bombs going off; my breath sounds like Darth Vader.

We creep up closer and I see the truck: it says "Forest Service." "Look," I whisper. "It's just Forest Service. That's okay, right?" hoping she'll say, *Right, it's totally fine, let's go chop wood.*

"Maybe," she says. "There's different kinds of rangers. Some of them are looking out for fires. But some of them are law enforcement." Two steps closer and I see their belts: they have guns. "Yup," she mutters. "Those are the cop kind."

My heart goes fast and fluttery, everything suddenly in super-sharp focus. My mind wants to run, but my muscles won't move.

"Stay still one sec," she says, pulling me behind a tree. "Let's see if we can hear them." I still can't see Jeff. Fuck.

The ranger cops lean over Nutmeg, pissed. One of them has a baton kind of thing on his belt and he keeps his hand there, threatening to pull it out. "Y'all need to get out of here," baton-cop says. The other one nods, muttering something I can't hear.

Nutmeg looks up at them, unblinking. He looks like a kid next to them. "We're not going anywhere."

"You will if we arrest you for trespassing," the ranger says.

I try to make myself invisible, unsure whether I'm more afraid of getting sent home or going to jail.

"You could, but you'd have to get me out of this," Nutmeg says, his arm sunk deep in. The ranger crouches down, his hand still on that baton.

"We can do that," he says. The look on his face reminds me of Jeff's dad.

Nutmeg is clenching his jaw, brave, defiant, but I know underneath it he has to be at least a little scared.

I turn to Sage. "We should do something."

"We go out there, they'll arrest us too. It won't help."

Then the ranger cop hits the dragon with his baton, trying to break it. Right by Nutmeg's head.

The noise cracks through the forest. Nutmeg buries his face in the dirt.

The cop hits the dragon three more times, each one harder than the next, each blow closer to Nutmeg's skull. It still doesn't break. "*Goddamn,*" the cop grunts, sweating, "this fucking thing," and motions to the other cop. "Hold his arm," he says. The other cop crouches down and pins Nutmeg's free arm.

Then the first cop rears back and punches Nutmeg. In the face. Nutmeg yells, I gasp, and Sage grips my shoulder hard. "Get the fuck out of there!" the ranger cop yells. "You hear me?!"

"I'm not going anywhere," Nutmeg says.

The cop punches him again. "You like that? Want me to fuck you up?"

Nutmeg doesn't move.

The cop kicks Nutmeg in the face, and suddenly blood is everywhere. I want to throw up.

It feels so wrong to stand here, hiding.

"Get up!" the cop yells.

"I told you, I'm not moving," Nutmeg yells, face blurred by the red of his blood.

I've never been afraid of cops before. I always thought, *Don't do anything wrong, they'll leave you alone. Protect you, even—keep you safe.* I always just assumed that the people in charge were taking care of everything, making sure it all ran right, that everyone was safe.

But that's not what's happening here. Not at all.

And they have guns.

The cop bends down and gets in Nutmeg's face, grabbing his hair. And then the other cop reaches under his uniform jacket, onto his belt. I look to Sage, panicked. But it's not a gun; it's this tiny can.

The cop points it at Nutmeg's face and sprays. And Nutmeg screams. I never knew why people described screams as "blood-curdling," but now I do.

"Pepper spray," Sage whispers.

"Get out of there!" the cop screams at Nutmeg again. Nutmeg's eyes squeeze shut, his body contorting around the pain. But he just shakes his head.

The two cops stand there for a second. And then one of them rears back and kicks Nutmeg in the ribs. I hear a sickening *crack*. Nutmeg moans, and spits blood into the dirt.

As they're getting into the truck, the cop says, "Tell your friends what happened to you. You've got three days to get out of here."

And then they drive away.

CHAPTER 15

Now it's dark and we're all back by the fire, burning up wood, trying to decide what to do. Everyone is here: Dirtrat, Stone and Cyn and silent Naya, Bender, Goat: they've emerged from their van-and-bus encampment, Popov on their breath, and they cluster with the rest of us, because now it's serious.

Jeff is with them. The Forest Service never even saw him: he spotted sirens through the trees, dropped his shovel half-way through a ditch, and ran.

He didn't holler up to Nutmeg first to warn him.

Doesn't matter, Nutmeg said when we all got back to camp, letting Jeff off the hook. *I woulda locked down any-way. Otherwise they would have gotten to the camp and shut all of us down. It's okay.* Nutmeg's face was marked with dirt, his cheek imprinted where it was pressed into the gravel. I remember that feeling on my own face, the lockdown, the refusal, the fear of it, and pride. I remember how Jeff looked at me when I locked in, admiring and jealous, like I was doing something that he couldn't do. That night I felt for him; I wanted to help him. But now I think: when it comes down to it, maybe he's the one who won't stand up, and not just because of his dad. Maybe he's not braver than me.

I look across the fire to him, sitting with the rowdy kids with their patches and piercings and vodka breath, interrupting each other, snickering or spacing out. I look around the spot where I'm sitting: Sage and Aaron and Exile focused, ready; Nutmeg wrapped in a blanket, bruised, black eyed, breathing shallow from a broken rib, saying, "I'm not going anywhere. I'm staying here." Jeff said, *What do you want? Just make a choice,* and I wonder if I already did.

"Three days," Aaron says. "That's not long. We need a plan." His voice is calm, but I can tell he's worried. I look to Sage, wanting her to reassure me or at least explain what's going on. But she just stares at the fire.

Sparks flick into our grubby faces, no one speaks up, and finally Aaron tells the group, "Look, Allie and I heard some shit in town a couple days ago." I see Jeff clock the *Allie* and hate it. I see purple-haired Cyn clock that and scowl at me.

"Apparently Cascade sees this as symbolic," Aaron goes on. "They think if they back down, it'll set some kind of precedent, and they're working on deals all over the state. So they have to keep going with the cut here, no matter what, to show that protesters won't stop them." Nutmeg and Exile nod, that same sober look Aaron had at the health food store. "They said three days till they come back. That means the rangers are planning to arrest us and clear out camp. That means we have to keep them from doing that. I think"—Aaron looks down—"I mean, obviously we all have to agree on the timing of this. But I think we should go ahead and set up the sit."

A murmur goes around the group. I don't know what a sit is, but Sage jumps in before I can ask. "It's too early," she says, shaking her head. "We aren't ready yet. We don't have ground support in town, nobody here's got climbing experience—"

"Yeah, but they're coming back, soon; we need to put it in motion."

Sage's voice gets hard. "Nobody here has training; we can't just blow that off. There are all kinds of risks. We're talking about putting someone in a three-hundred-foot tree."

Oh. A tree sit. They want to put someone in Legacy so they can't cut her down, so that if anybody tried to, they'd be cutting down a person. I heard about tree sits once on Independent World News, parked outside the school with Jeff in Grandpa. I think we were maybe making out. That seems so far off, like a million years ago.

"Seriously," Sage says. She looks across the fire at the kids from the buses. "Any of you guys ever been up in a tree?"

"We occupied an oak at U of O campus once," Goat says. "It was like forty feet, maybe?"

"Bullshit." Stone laughs, giving Goat a friendly punch on the shoulder. "You made some flyers, dude."

"Or, I mean, some people I know occupied it," Goat says, then punches Stone back. "I dropped out, so." The guys laugh. Sage just looks at the rest of us like, *See what I mean?*

"Okay, fine, but you got another idea?" Aaron asks her. "'Cause, I mean, they just broke Nutmeg's rib. They're coming in, and they're coming in to cut. I don't think we can rely on the dragons, and the ditches aren't done." He shoots Jeff an accusatory look. Aaron's eyes glint green in the fire. It's the first time I've ever seen him anything but calm.

"No, I don't," Sage bristles. "But that doesn't mean we should just blow off the risk. You and I are organizers, we've never been up. Exile and Nutmeg know about barricades and road stuff. Until we can get some people here who've set up a sit before, who have actually been up, I don't think it's safe, and I don't think we're ready, and I think we should be coming up with something else."

Everybody squirms; no one wants Sage and Aaron to be fighting. They're the closest thing to someone who's in charge. "I've been around a lot of sits." Nutmeg tries to break the tension. "I can rig on the ground; I could probably figure out how to apply that up high."

"Yeah, but they probably broke your rib," Sage tells Nutmeg. "We can't send you up."

"Fine," Aaron says. "I'll do it." Sage looks at Aaron like, *What the hell are you talking about? We didn't talk about that.*

"Look." He turns to her. "I think it's necessary. I know knots, I've got endurance, Nutmeg can figure out how to rig pretty much anything, you and Exile are good for strategy. Other folks can do ground support, whatever. It'll work."

"I'm not cool with that," Sage says. "I'm sorry, I'm just not."

"They're coming in three days," he says.

She just looks at him.

"Okay," Aaron says, "let's take it off of you and me. Let's take a vote." He turns to the group. "Who all thinks I should go up?"

Nutmeg and Exile raise their hands. So do all the school-bus kids. Jeff looks at me; I'm sitting on my hands. He raises his.

Sage eyes me. I can tell she really doesn't want Aaron to go up. I look back and forth between the two of them, Aaron with his hand in the air, and even though everyone else already voted, I feel this pressure, like it's somehow up to me.

"It's the best thing for Legacy, Al," Aaron says, and finally I put my hand up too.

I feel sort of sick to my stomach. But it's not like me saying something would change anything.

"Fine," Sage says. "I just want to say I think we're not prepared, and I don't think it's safe. But I'm not going to stand in the way of the group." I watch her, sussing out whether she really means it. Her eyes are clear, honest. I think she does. I relax a little. I didn't fuck it up by raising my hand. I'm pretty sure it's okay.

"Okay." Aaron takes a breath. "Everybody better go to bed. There's gonna be a lot to do starting at sunrise."

Exile goes to get ashes to put out the campfire; people start to disperse. I brush myself off and look across the fire, waiting for Jeff to walk back to our tent. He's got his back to me; Goat and Dirtrat busted out a bowl. I stare at his back, his thermal shirt tracing the V from his shoulders to his waist. I can't look at him without knowing how it feels to touch him. It's not right that he's ignoring me.

"Jeff," I finally say. "Hey."

He turns, orange flickering on his cheeks, his lip ring glinting in the light. "I'm gonna hang out for a while," he says. "Don't stress if I crash in the bus," and he turns back around.

"Oh," I say, half to myself. *Crash: that's overnight.* "Okay." And I walk back to our tent alone.

The next morning there's a ton of stuff to get, and we have to get it fast. Milk crates, carabiners, metal clamps. Tarps and plastic, water bottles, plywood, yards of rope. We've got hammers and batteries and nails, but that's about it. Someone has to go to town.

Jeff didn't come back to our tent last night. I don't know what that means, or how to talk about it; every time it elbows into my mind, my pulse races and I feel queasy. Is he trying to tell me something? Was he with Cyn?

I don't know the rules: I never had a boyfriend before Jeff. The closest thing was Andy's friends, and they weren't close at all. Jeff and I have never been "official"—we both just always only had each other. If he'd ever asked me to "be his girlfriend," it would've been bizarre, because I already was. Ever since we've been around other people, though, I've been confused. He got mad that I didn't tell him I was going to town with Aaron, but he doesn't tell me everything he's doing, and now he's hardly even talking to me. Last night he slept somewhere else. With a girl who hasn't talked to me, not once. I'm pissed at him—but underneath the mad is a raw layer of hurt, and underneath that an empty hole of fear: without him, I'm cut loose. When I think about it, it feels bottomless.

I try to just keep working. Aaron and Exile are headed into town, and I ask if I can go. I'm not telling Jeff.

This time that's on purpose.

As we're loading into the car, Sage comes up to Aaron. He looks at her, and I can tell he's not sure what she'll say to him. But nobody's yelling, nobody's hiding; it's more like they both know there's a problem, and they're both there to figure it out. I've never seen that before. Like: things can be hard with someone, and you can work them out. I never saw anybody do that. My mom never worked anything out. My dad just left.

Sage hands Aaron a mobile phone, big and blocky.

"Here," she says. "See if you can get a signal in town, make some calls to people who will get the word out. If we're going up, I at least want to build some ground support."

Aaron nods. "Makes sense." He looks at her a minute, his face softening. She looks back at him. It's like she's giving him permission. I see it pass between them. "Thank you," he says. She holds on to his hand. It's nice. I think, *That's how it's supposed to be.*

Aaron drives as the sun finishes coming up; I sit in the back-seat of Exile's car, picking at the peeling upholstery, listening to the guys talk.

"I don't know how many dumpsters we're gonna find; this town is pretty small," Aaron tells Exile. "I think we're gonna have to hit a store. But we don't want to draw attention."

"Do we want to send Alison in?"

"I think a girl buying plywood here will draw more atten-tion than either of us," Aaron says. "They'd probably just assume we're carpenters, but she'd set alarm bells off." It's weird to think about that: at the Free State I've been doing all that kind of stuff. Building, digging, whatever. But this is the real world, I guess, and a small town, and plywood and carpentry aren't normal for girls. It almost makes me mad: I shouldn't have to be a "girl," I should be allowed to just be a *person.*

Aaron pulls into an alley near a big green dumpster and we get out of the car. He leaves the engine idling, doors unlocked.

They lift the plastic lid off and clamber up, both of them old hands at this. I stand on the damp pavement, unsure what I'm supposed to do, till Exile says, "C'mon," and reaches out his hand. I grab it, lift myself clumsily up into the dumpster, and then we're sitting in a pile of trash. I look at us and see street urchins, orphans from some eighth-grade book for English class—rags, patches, garbage—and I wonder what the hell anyone who knew me before would say. My mom, Andy, anyone from school. Would they even recognize me? I'm grubby and unwashed, hiding from store owners, going through somebody's trash. So we can find stuff to build an illegal platform a hundred feet in the sky. That somebody is going to live on.

I hold my breath against the smell and dig in. Once you get past the layer of gross, it's amazing how much good stuff people throw away. Sure enough, we find broken two-by-fours; sheets of plastic, empty jugs. Down the alley two plastic milk crates sit at a convenience store's back door. As we're picking them up, we hear footsteps from inside; we look at each other and run, laughing, back to the car. We tumble in before they can see us, and for a second I feel wild, free, the thrill of getting away with it. Together. Wood scraps press into my lap, hard edges and sharp angles, but I don't care.

Aaron smooths his hair into a neater ponytail before he walks into the hardware store. Exile and I stay in the car.

"So—do you know how to do this?" I ask him. "Build it, I mean."

"Not really," he says. "I mean, I know the basic idea. But I've never done it myself."

"Is Sage right—do you think it's dangerous?"

"Well, I mean, dangerous compared to what? Compared to sitting at home watching TV, sure. Compared to being outside in a hurricane? Maybe not." It's not particularly comforting that the only thing he can think of that's worse is being in a *hurricane*. "Way I see it is, you spend too much time being scared, it'll slow you down and they win." He looks at me. "'Cause they're not scared."

"But they've got everything. I mean, cops, money—we don't have any of that."

"Yeah, but there are a lot of people out there who'd support us."

I think of Tacoma, kids at school, the people at my mom's job. I'm not so sure that's true. "You think?" I ask.

"I do."

That thought has never occurred to me: that anyone out there could support me, that I might not be as alone as I thought. Well, it did once. Looking at that Antioch catalog, getting that acceptance letter, I thought, *Maybe that's a place full of weirdos like me, people who were alone where they came from and now they can be together.* But that's just an idea. I've never trusted it could actually be true.

We drive back to the Free State, sheets of plywood hanging out the trunk, straining against the rope. For a second I let myself believe what Exile said about the world: that there are other people out there. And even though the car is weighted down, for a minute I feel light. For a minute, I feel like the world could be bigger than I thought it was. And that makes me think maybe I don't need Jeff as much as I thought I did.

When we get back, I don't look for him. I push him out of my head, unpack the gear, load it onto my shoulders. I'm panting and it's heavy, but I like the work. I fold up tarps and dropcloths, finish fast, and holler off, "What's next?"

"Maybe fill some more food buckets up?" Aaron says. "Or blankets, I'll need blankets. There are extras over by the tents." Everybody's working, even Goat and Stone and Bender, even Dirtrat. They're probably high, and working slow, but they're still doing stuff. There's that much to do.

The sun sinks past the tree line by the time we have everything organized; then we have to hike it to Legacy. We load up like pack mules, plastic bags and milk crates and backpacks, cords of wood lashed together with bungee cords. Jeff stays away from me, hiking with the school-bus kids and Cyn. They lag behind us. I keep turning around to see if he'll try to catch up with me, but he doesn't.

By the time we're done, the sun is setting. We have to get back to camp: you can't cook in the dark, and everybody's starving.

"Are we just leaving all this stuff here?" Sage asks. "I don't think that's smart."

"She's right," Aaron says. "They might be watching,"

and I think *really?* "We went to town twice; people saw us. And I put the word out for support. If they're gearing up, they probably have an eye on us. We leave supplies out overnight, they might get swiped."

"You're right," Nutmeg says.

"Someone's gotta sleep out here," Sage says. "I'd volunteer, but—" She looks to Aaron. I can tell she wants to stay with him. He's going up tomorrow. For a second I feel jealous, a sharp twinge in my chest. I'm sure I'll be alone again in the tent tonight, staring at the stars through the mesh, waiting to see if Jeff will come back from the bus, waking up in the morning to find that he hasn't.

"I'll do it," I jump in, not even looking at Jeff.

It's like the first night we were out here, when I volunteered to lock down—but instead of doing it to make him feel better, this time I'm doing it to say, *Fuck you. I can be alone, and you can't hurt me.*

Jeff looks at me, quick, a flicker of hurt. My heart flutters—is he going to stop me? Do I want him to? And then Cyn catches his eye and he catches hers, and he leans back on his heels, adjusts his stocking cap, and whatever was open between us for a second gets locked up again.

Fine.

echoes through the branches. "I got the spot!" There's a pause, and then he yells a little softer, "It's beautiful up here, you guys."

"You locked in?" Exile yells up.

"Yup!" he yells back. The rope pokes through the branches, coming down toward us. When it hits the ground, Nutmeg latches the rope to a sheet of plywood. And then there's a grunt from way above us, and the plywood lifts.

Aaron hauls the platform up slowly, catching it on branches as it goes. He gets it all the way up to where he is, unhooks it, then lowers the rope again. The milk crate full of tools goes up next, then Aaron's pack, then the other sheets of wood. Finally he hollers down, ragged, "I can't lift anything else, you guys. My arms are shaking. I gotta rest."

We all stop staring up for the first time and look at each other. He's up there. The sheets of wood are up there. The tools are up there. I feel his absence down here like a missing tooth, the hole where he used to be almost more noticeable than his presence was. The balance feels different.

CHAPTER 17

That night I sleep by myself in the tent, and for the first time I'm not wondering if Jeff will come back; I know he won't. It's his third night in the bus and I'm sure something is going on with him and Cyn, and I know he won't talk to me about it unless I make him. *Coward,* I think.

And then I realize: maybe that's what we had in common. *Cowards.* Maybe that's why we've never been official: we've both been too scared. Maybe we just closed ourselves together in his car, in his basement, cocooned together in a private world where we never had to talk about things and we didn't have to be alone. Maybe now I want to talk about things. Maybe now I'm not so scared.

The next day is the last day before the cops said they'd come back. No one stronger's looking out for us. There's no one to protect us but each other. It's all on us. The whole camp has this nervous energy: there's nothing to do, Aaron's up there, all we can do is wait. But none of us knows what will happen when they come.

That morning Exile and I hike out to Legacy to send up water. When Aaron lowers the crate back down, there's a note. *It's beautiful. You can see for miles: other mountains, even town. Town is tiny compared with everything. It's so quiet. It's like another world. Except it's this one, right here. It's our world. Take care of it. I started making calls today. Keep an eye on the papers; there should be stories coming out. Tell Sage I miss her. Or better yet, just show her this: I miss you, Sage.*

Reading that last line, my throat catches. I cough to cover it so Exile won't notice. We take the milk crate and the empty jug, and we head back to camp.

I haven't talked to Jeff in, like, four days. It's starting to get stupid. And it's the last day before the rangers are supposed to come and clear us out, and I'm starting to actually give a shit what happens. At first I was working hard so I wouldn't have to think about my mom or school or Andy. After that I was working hard so I wouldn't have to think about Jeff. But somewhere in there I started to actually care about all this. Nutmeg got his rib broken; Aaron is hundreds of feet off the ground; Sage, who never gets scared, is scared for him. There's something here to protect, something worth protecting, and there's nobody who's gonna do it but us. The school-bus kids are too caught up in themselves to be useful; I don't want to be like them. I don't want weird shit between Jeff and me to distract me. I want to be able to help when it's time.

I head back to the bus, parked in a clearing away from the tents. The top of it's covered with pine needles now, rain rusting the edges where the paint's peeled back. I haven't been in here for a couple of weeks, not since that night I tried to hang out with Jeff and them, and Stone pulled that creepy shit with me and Jeff didn't even notice and I had to leave.

There are curtains on the windows; I can't see in. I walk up to the closed doors, suddenly feeling like I'm in elementary school at the bus stop, not sure who's on board, if anyone will let me sit with them. I knock.

After a minute, the doors open; pot smoke billows out. It's Cyn, wearing a dirty wifebeater and no bra, her purple hair faded to a gross yellowish lavender. She looks at me, mean like Naomi fucking Gladstone. "Hey," she says. "What do you want?"

"I want to talk to Jeff." I'm not positive he's there, but I can guess.

"Jeff!" she hollers back, annoyed. Good guess. She just stands there, staring, while I wait for him. She chews on her lip ring. I think she's trying to intimidate me. I'm not scared of her, though. That's new.

Finally Jeff comes out, pulling on his black hoodie, the one with the patch, the one he was wearing that first day we met at Point Defiance Park. I suddenly feel really sad about that hoodie. It's ridiculous, I know, but everything's changed, and the few things that are familiar suddenly matter. There aren't many left.

"Come for a walk with me," I say. "I want to talk to you."

Cyn watches as we walk away, and then she goes back into the bus.

I take him back to where we saw the deer, in the forest, on the way to Legacy. We both know the trail now. I think part of me hopes the place will magically erase the last couple of weeks, so Jeff and I are back on that sun-dappled, quiet day, so I don't have to say the things I know I have to.

When we get there, I look at the ground. Out of the corner of my eye I see him watching me. Out here, he looks smaller. But he's still angry. I can feel it rising off him in waves. I am too.

"So?" he finally says. "You brought me back here, you must have something to say."

"I do," I say. My heart is beating hard. I look into his eyes for some flicker of what used to be there, but all I see is far away. "I don't know how to say it . . ."

"Say what?" he says, his eyes hard and his cheekbones sharp. "I came all the way out here with you. You want to talk to me, talk to me," he says, impatient. "Otherwise I'm going." My face flushes. He doesn't have the right to talk to me that way.

"Okay, fine, then," I snap back, and then it tumbles out. "You know what I think? I think you're jealous of Aaron.

You've been pissy at me ever since we started hanging out." He looks away. A flicker of feeling shows through his icy eyes, flashes under his set jaw. "Sage is his girlfriend. Nothing happened. You're the one who's got another fucking girlfriend. I didn't do anything wrong. It isn't fair. You're being an asshole to me, like I did something horrible, and I didn't do anything wrong."

He looks stunned. I just keep going: "It's fucked up, what you did. It's fucked up you acted like there was some rule that said I have to tell you where I'm going, and it's fucked up you made me feel like shit for not knowing what to say, and I'm fucking sorry, okay, I'm sorry I don't always know what to say or what to do, but you know what? You don't either, and it's not like you're so fucking brave." It all rushes out at once, and when it's over, I'm shocked I said it. I've never talked that way to anyone except my mom the night I left.

He just stands there, fists stuffed in his hoodie pockets, dwarfed by the forest, looking at the ground. I want him to say he's sorry. I want him to realize that it's true: that he was being a dick. And now that I've said all that, I want him to feel as raw and scared and open as I do right now.

But he looks away, and then he shrugs, and says, "Okay. If that's the way you feel."

"What do you mean, 'if that's the way you feel'? If that's the way I feel what?"

"If that's the way you feel, we're breaking up. I mean we already kind of did."

That's what I came out here for. It was my choice; I was fine with it. I know that.

But now that we're here, somehow it's different. Something in me crumples.

"Yeah," I say, "we are," and it's all gone, the last piece of home that was left, the last thing that felt familiar, and I feel more alone than I can remember in a long, long time.

I tell him I want to be in the forest for a while. The truth is I don't want to cry in front of him.

While he hikes back, I walk deeper in, toward Legacy. After a minute I hit a fork I haven't seen before. I stop and scan the trees, trying to figure out which way to go. I track the shapes of the branches, the knots in the trunks: the one on the right has a big gnarled branch twisting out, and I finally recognize it. I wonder if this is how Andy felt on those Scout trips, in the woods with a compass, finding his way, while I was at home with our mom and dad. Andy always seemed so sure that he'd be able to find his way anywhere. I wonder if this is how he got that way.

When I get to Legacy, I look up at the ropes, the platform so high up it's just a tiny dot. I wish I could talk to Aaron, but it's too far. I put my arms around the trunk. It's a fucking cliché, I feel ridiculous, but I need to hold on to something. I've got nothing left.

I tell myself, *You've done this before.* I was alone when Andy died, when my mom fell out from under us, when my dad left. It's not like I'm not used to it. I give my weight over to the tree, collapse into it, let something bigger than me hold me up. I used to lean into Andy like this, when I was little and he was already tall. He was never embarrassed, never acted annoyed; he just stood there, strong, and wrapped his arms around me. Like he knew what to do. Like he was stronger than me, and he was looking out for everything, making sure it all ran right, protecting me. The moss on her trunk is like velvet; I feel wet on my cheek. At first I think it's dew, but it's too warm for that, and suddenly I realize that I'm crying.

I stay that way a long time, till the red fades from my eyes and the hitch subsides, before I'm ready to head back to camp.

The rest of the day everyone just waits. They said *three days*; this is the third. That could mean the rangers are coming tonight, or tomorrow. We'll hear the engines down the mountain, and when we do, we'll all lock down, so they can't arrest us. There's a whole row of dragons now, and a bunch of Kryptonite bike locks; lock one of those around your neck, attach it to a steering wheel or a wheel well, and they can't cut you out. We'll stay locked in till they leave, and then again when they come back, and then again until they leave us alone. I don't want to think about that. I want to keep working. I want to do things. I want something to throw myself into, people to work with, so I can feel not alone, so I can stay here, in this moment, instead of spinning off into futures and lockdowns and arrests, what happens afterward and home. Wherever that is. I chop more wood with Sage and then I help Nutmeg check the dragons and then I find a shovel and finish the ditches that Jeff never did. I stay far, far away from the bus.

By noon the next day no one has come and we're all starting to wonder if those newspaper stories Aaron mentioned ran and the cops decided to hold off. Sage starts to relax, like maybe she was worried for nothing, and I see her smiling again.

By one o'clock we decide we don't all need to stay near the dragons and Exile and I can hike to bring Aaron fresh water. We send it up the ropes in the crate, and when it lowers back down, there's another note. *Spoke with lawyers from Pacific Land Protection Council—turns out Cascade's permission to log has an expiration date. The current permit only has two more weeks on it, and then they have to reapply for everything. If we can hold them off that long, these trees will be safe for a good while. PCLC is glad I'm up here—it slows things down. It's enough just to slow things down, for now. We made the right decision. I miss you, Sage.*

Exile gives a little happy yelp when we read that, and we practically sprint back to camp. This might be working. The whole thing. It might be enough to slow things down; if we just stop the bad things from happening, maybe good people will come in and figure out how to make it better. Exile might be right: there might be people out there who support us.

What we do might matter. They might actually not cut down this forest and that amazing tree. Because of us.

That night we stay up late around the fire, happy. Sage holds my hand and says, "Good job," and I feel like I'm a part of something, and when I go back to the tent, I look up at the orange cords and the green fabric, and I think of Andy inside it as a kid, out on his trips. I imagine him looking up at the ceiling of it, the same ceiling I'm looking at now, and feeling safe, and strong, and like he can find his way, and for the first time it's okay with me that I'm alone in here.

CHAPTER 18

When the noise comes, it's not even sunrise. I startle awake under the half-dark sky, heart racing, confused. *What time is it? Am I dreaming? Did I even sleep?* But then the sound starts up again, loud like a construction site, and I rub my eyes awake. I look out my mesh window and see other shapes in the predawn dark, everyone sitting up and stirring.

"Those are chain saws," Nutmeg whisper-yells across the forest floor. "We must've slept through the engines. They're already up here. They got past the dragons. And it's not rangers. Those are loggers."

I've never moved so fast, so silently, in my entire life. It feels like we're animals, or in a war. Adrenaline runs up my spine; my breath is shallow. My foot crunches a stick beneath me and I flinch at the noise, wishing against gravity, hating the heavy realness of my body, wanting to be wind. "Shhhh," Sage hisses. "Don't let them hear we're over here," and I nod at her: I can't speak to say, *I'm sorry*.

When we're dressed, Sage gathers us into a huddle. The chain saws—now I know that's what they are—echo into the forest, grinding mechanical wails ramping up, crescendoing, then dropping into silence. They're not far off. "Okay," she says under her breath when the saws slow down enough. "Cascade didn't wait for the cops to clear us out. That gives us information."

The saws ramp up again, roaring into my ears. It's terrifying how loud they are, how close. "What kind of information?" I yell over the noise.

"What?" Sage yells back. I only know because I can read her lips.

"*What kind of information?*" I yell again, but she shakes her head: it's hopeless.

The cut stops for a second and she says, "It tells us they're in a rush; they're trying to scare us out and cut it all before the permit's up. Motherfuckers." Her jaw clenches. She looks like someone out of a movie, fierce, with her tattoos and her muddy tank top and her muscles and her fists.

Suddenly something crashes down a hundred yards away. I almost jump out of my skin: the noise is huge, like a car crash or a building falling. And I realize: if we were closer, that could have fallen onto us.

"Fuck. That's a branch," Nutmeg says. "They're stripping down a tree. Once they get the big branches down, they'll make a run at the trunk. We need to stop this before that happens."

Stop it? I think. *How the hell do we do that?*

Sage looks at him, eyes blazing like an animal. "What's the plan." She says it like a command.

"Let's start with where they are, and where we are," he says. "Sounds like a hundred yards south. That means they're away from Legacy, at least. What's between them and her grove? Anybody hiked it?"

"I have," I pipe up. "It's pretty dense. The path is narrow; there's a bunch of boulders there."

"Good," he says. "That's good. Boulders are hard for them to get equipment past. That buys us time."

"But they'll keep cutting in the meantime, wherever they can," Sage says. "We've gotta block them, wherever they are."

"There could be rangers out there, though," Exile says. "If we get too close, they'll arrest us."

"I'm not afraid of getting arrested," Jeff says, loud. Dirtrat slinks backward like he might be. So do the other bus kids. Stone is at the back of the pack of them, not looking at anyone. It's amazing: on the bus he's the loudest and the drunkest, the one who gets the cigarettes, the ringleader. Out here when real shit is happening, he makes himself invisible. He's even standing behind Dirtrat. This shit brings out your true colors, I guess.

"It's not about being afraid," Sage tells Jeff, firm. "It doesn't matter if we're scared or not. What matters is what we do. It's not strategic. If we let them arrest us, they'll just come in and cut, and we won't be here to block them."

And then the chain saws roar up again.

The dragons are useless; the trucks already got past. We just have to block their access to as much of the forest as we can. Nutmeg and Sage and I are going to jerry-rig a rope blockade between where the loggers are and Legacy. Sage has a Swiss Army knife; Nutmeg takes a big length of rope. "Grab that other one," he tells me, and I'm wrapping up the heavy rope when Jeff reaches into the gear pile and grabs a bike chain.

"Here." Jeff hands the chain to Goat, and then another one to Dirtrat. "They're good and heavy."

"What are you doing?" Nutmeg asks him.

Jeff doesn't answer. A chain saw ramps up into a roar, close to us. My eardrums throb.

"*What are you doing?*" I yell at Jeff. He doesn't answer.

And then there's a thunderous crack, the loudest noise I've ever heard, and then a creak, and a tree crashes onto the forest floor. It's not close enough to see, but it's huge, and it's ancient, something that shouldn't be cut down. The ground shakes beneath my feet like an earthquake.

"Doesn't sound like they're gonna stop on their own," Jeff shouts. "So we're going to stop them."

"That's crazy," Sage yells as a chain saw ramps up again.

"You're gonna go try to stop them? That puts all of us in danger. Do you even know how many loggers there are? Or if there are rangers? You wanna get arrested?"

"Dirtrat climbed a tree and checked it out while you were talking." Jeff spits the word, like talking is a bad thing. "It's just the loggers. And yeah, we're gonna stop them." He wraps the chain around his hand. The saws quiet for a moment.

Jeff takes a step toward me. "Last chance, Alison," he says. "You wanna stand up?" He says it mean, like if I don't go with him, I'm a coward.

Sage looks straight at me. "We need you here, Alison."

We need you. Nobody's ever said that to me before.

The saws ramp up again and Jeff moves closer to the noise, still watching me.

"Don't do it," Nutmeg yells at him over the grinding, angrier and more urgent than I've heard him. "It's stupid. And it's dangerous. You could get killed." And then another thundering crack, and another tree falls. Closer this time. I feel the crash through my whole body.

"Might be dangerous," Jeff says, "but at least it's fucking brave." Then he, Goat, and Dirtrat head off.

My chest is tied in knots, but there's no time to think about it. I can't stop him. I can't go after him. He's gone. I turn back to Nutmeg and Sage. "What do we do?"

Sage cranes her neck. "Goddamn it," she says as they turn into tiny dots, then disappear behind tree trunks. "They just screwed us."

"Look, we don't know yet," Nutmeg says. "We don't know how the loggers will react. Maybe they'll stay calm. That can happen—"

"Are they gonna get hurt? Or arrested?" I interrupt, my heart pounding in my throat. It's bizarre: I'm so pissed at Jeff. It's his own fault, but I still want to make sure he's okay.

"Maybe," Nutmeg says. "But there's nothing we can do. They left. Following them won't do any good. We'd just put ourselves in the line of fire."

A big branch crashes through the leaves and hits the ground, echoing, and a logger yells.

"Okay," I finally say, my heart twisting in my chest. "You guys have the rope? Let's go."

We find the widest part of the trail, the two strongest trees flanking the path. Nutmeg knows a million kinds of knots, ones Andy learned for Eagle Scouts but a lot of others, too: clove hitch, bowline, Bachmann, stevedore. Sage cuts the ropes and Nutmeg ties them fast, making a kind of web to stretch across the trail. The top line is eight feet off the ground; when it's finished, he says, we can tie ourselves in up there. If the loggers try to cut the web, the whole thing won't unravel.

Even working fast, even with three of us, it takes a long time to build an eight-by-ten-foot net. My hands are raw from rope burn when we hear yelling up the trail, and then a crash. We all stop moving instantly. I can make out Jeff's voice, and Dirtrat's, but I can't hear what they're saying.

Then another male voice, angry; it isn't Goat. And another crash—it sounds like branches breaking—and then running, toward us, and the voices getting louder.

"Shit," Sage says. "What the hell is going on?" She folds up the knife and jams it into her pocket. Boots crash through branches fifty yards away.

"What should I do?" I turn to Sage and Nutmeg, praying that they know.

"Duck down," Nutmeg says, pointing to a boulder. "Behind that rock. I'll be over here. Don't move—no sound."

I nod and crouch behind the boulder. Nutmeg gets behind a tree, and Sage behind another, farther up. We leave the rope web hanging there, half finished; there's no time to hide it. The voices get louder. They're not on the path. They're running through the woods, stepping on the underbrush, bushwhacking through brambles, and a logger's chasing after them.

"You little shit!" the logger yells; it's the first thing I can make out. "You give me that!" And then, squinting, I see Jeff hurtling through the branches, Goat and Dirtrat right behind him, a blue bag gripped tight under his arm. It says "Cascade." He's got the logger's gear.

My thighs are burning, but I know I can't move. I grit my teeth and lean against the rough side of the rock, trying to lessen the pressure.

They run past, then the logger. The logger is fat and fortyish, but also mad and strong, so he's gaining on the guys.

Jeff yells, "Ha ha, fucker!" and I think, *What the fuck are you doing?* as hard as I can, straining my brain to yell at him telepathically.

The guys pass us, running to another part of the forest, outside Cascade's permit range. That's what they're doing: they're trying to lure the loggers away from the cut.

As they get farther away, their words blur from the distance. We can't see what's happening, and there's no way of finding out. I feel helpless, and it's crazy that people lived like this for hundreds of thousands of years, without being able to communicate unless they were face-to-face. It's like we're animals.

After a few minutes, it seems safe to come out. Sage crawls over to Nutmeg, motions for me to come too. We're about to start work on the rope barricade again when we hear another yell. But this time it's coming from over by Legacy.

CHAPTER 19

We stop and listen for a second, unsure whether we actually heard what we thought we did. Then it comes again. "*SAGE!*"

It's Aaron's voice.

Sage freezes; then she turns and runs. I zigzag behind her through the woods, trying not to lose sight of her as she darts through the forest. She's quick as a fox. "*SAGE!*" It gets louder as we get closer, and then we're near enough to see: someone's up there with Aaron in the tree.

"Fuck." Sage stares at the platform, her mouth open. "Holy Christ."

There's a climber in the platform, roped into his own harness. He's got a yellow vest and a hard hat and fancy climbing lanyards. And he's big.

He's wrestling Aaron down.

"They're trying to get me out!" Aaron yells, his voice

ragged with fear. "This is Cascade! They're trying to unhook me!"

His body looks limp. "Is he hurt?" I ask Sage, panicked.

"You go limp to make it harder for them to move you. But I don't know if he's hurt. He could be." She wrings her hands, terrified. "*Fuck.*" She looks up again. "Are you hurt, Aaron?" she yells.

"He's trying to untie me!" Aaron says. "Get a camera from camp—this needs to be filmed! It's evidence!"

"I'm not going back there!" Sage shouts up. "I'm not leaving you!"

We hear thuds from high up in the tree; knocked-off bark hits the forest floor.

"Who's there with you?" Aaron calls.

"Just me and Alison," she screams, her voice raw.

"Send Allie—" he grunts, and then there's another thud.

I look at Sage: Is he serious? I'm supposed to leave them out here, Sage alone and Aaron getting wrestled out of his ropes two hundred feet above the forest floor?

"There's nothing we can do from down here," she says to me. "There's a video camera in my backpack, in my tent. You're helping him by getting it. Just go."

I stand there, frozen. "*Run,*" she says. "*GO,*" and finally I do.

I run faster than I have my whole entire life; I don't even feel my body working, I just feel like wind. I rip Sage's bag apart, throwing her stuff everywhere; her camera's at the bottom. I pocket it and run out, leaving her tent flap open behind me. Exile's at the fire circle; other people too; they're all a blur. "What's going on?" Exile asks.

"Cascade's in the tree with Aaron," I shout as I run past them, my eyes pinned forward as I race out of camp and skid down the trail.

By the time I get back there, two guys are in the tree with him. The other one's taller, with the same hard hat, same vest. "The other one came from behind," Sage says, her gaze not moving off Aaron. "They must have another trail cut. I didn't see him till he was halfway up the trunk." Tears and sweat cut clean swaths through the dirt on her cheeks.

More grunts come from above, more falling bark. I have to squint to see Aaron. His blue T-shirt is barely visible through the thicket of branches, behind the hulking vested bodies of the Cascade climbers, working hard to pin him down. The platform and branches block our view; we can only get glimpses.

"Set the camera on video and zoom the lens as close in as you can," Sage barks at me. "We'll need everything."

I do what she says, but it feels sick. Aaron is up there, getting beat up, and I'm standing here *filming* it? I need to help him, not just watch.

"Sage," I say. "I have to do something. Can we get up there?"

She shakes her head. "There's nothing we can do but stay

here and talk to him, do what he asks. We're witnesses. Get a record. That's a job."

I hear running in the woods behind us, and then people from camp burst into the clearing, everyone's shouts a jumble. I don't even look at them, trying to keep my camera arm steady. It's shaking, like the rest of me.

"*What's going on?*" "*Who's up there with him?*" "*Is he hurt?*" Everybody yells at once, peppering us with questions till Sage yells, "QUIET!" and everyone shuts up.

"Two climbers from Cascade," she says. "They're trying to get him down. He's resisting. Now, everyone shut up so we can hear what's happening up there."

People do what she says, even Dirtrat, even Jeff.

There's another crash from the branches, and then a thunk that sounds like something hitting the platform. Maybe someone's head. "You okay?" Sage shouts up, urgent.

"I'm all right," Aaron yells. "That was my boot."

"What's going on?" Sage pleads. "You have to let us know what's happening!"

"Okay," Aaron yells down. Then some more sounds of struggling, then, "Okay. They're trying to get me out of here. The shorter guy says his name is Dan, the other one is Ox. Ox has his boot on my chest right now—"

"We're trying to keep him safe, ma'am," a different voice shouts down from the tree, cutting Aaron off. "This is a rescue operation."

"Rescue?!" Sage rages back. "That's bullshit! He's two

hundred feet off the ground and you've got your boot on his chest!"

"This is a safety issue," the guy repeats. "He's endangered himself by putting himself up here on company property. Now he's endangering us by resisting."

"Don't listen to them, Sage!" Aaron yells. "They're doing all kinds of dangerous shit up here; the one guy shoved me, and they've got my feet hog-tied."

"You fuckers!" Sage screams at them. "Let him go!"

"We can't let him go, ma'am. He's putting himself in danger—"

"*They're* putting me in danger, Sage! They're doing it!"

I look to Sage, panicking. Every muscle in my body wants to move, wants to run to that tree and claw my way up it. Blood is pounding through my veins.

She doesn't take her eyes off Aaron. "Keep filming."

"I've got a lockbox up here," Aaron yells.

"Don't talk about that!" Sage interrupts.

"They already saw it; I'm not giving anything away," Aaron yells back. "They made it up here before I could lock in to the box properly, but I'm still working on it. They've got a lotta my ropes undone, but if I can get my harness hooked in good enough, they won't be able to get me down."

"No! He can't do that—" Nutmeg blurts, but Sage cuts him off.

"*Shh*, let him finish. He's got a plan."

Above us, Aaron thrashes in the grip of the climbers. His

shoulders come off the platform, hanging over thin air. I can see his red hair through the branches. "Shit! Hang on," he yells. Then he squirms back onto the wood.

One of the climbers yells, "Young man, you are putting yourself in danger. Stop moving." Then: "STOP MOVING!" The businesslike tone leaves the climber's voice and suddenly he sounds like a guy in a bar brawl.

"Okay," Aaron pants. "I'm close. If I can hook in to the lockbox, we'll be good. I just have to unhook my harness for a second—"

"NO! DON'T DO THAT!" Sage screams, eyes bulging.

Nutmeg overlaps fast: "That's what I thought he meant. He'll have to unhook to get into the lockbox. Nothing will be holding him to the tree. DON'T DO IT!" Nutmeg yells up to Aaron. "IT ISN'T SAFE!"

I'm frozen, heartbeat like a drum in my ears. My arm is shaking so bad I can hardly hold the camera. I taste metal in my mouth.

"I'm close—" Aaron says. "Six inches—" and then more dirt and bark fall from above, more thuds and thunks and banging on the platform—and then a sickening *CRACK*.

Aaron's body hits the branch below the platform, then bounces up like a rag doll.

"FUCK!" Nutmeg shouts. "Is he tied in? Can anybody see if he's still got his harness on?!" Sage is hyperventilating.

Through the branches, Aaron keeps falling. He's scream-

I wake up before sunrise the next morning, black sky turning blue above me. Rain falls soft from the sky, patters on the forest floor, most of it caught by the trees. It's quiet. Really quiet: no one else is awake yet back at camp.

And I realize: I'm okay.

I hardly slept last night, blinking in the dark, ears attuned to every sound. But finally I must've fallen asleep. And here I am, and here are the supplies, still safe. I feel kind of hard, and kind of hollow, but also kind of proud.

I rub my eyes and sit up. Today's the day. I look up the huge trunk, darkened by the rain. It's like climbing a skyscraper. It's hard to imagine Aaron up there. I know there's a way to get up, but I can't picture it. I wonder if he feels like I did last night: scared but pushing past it, shaking inside but forcing yourself to do it anyway. I wonder if Sage is holding his hand, helping him feel better. I feel that twinge again, a vacuum inside me that keeps trying to suck me in. I have to get up and get to work.

By daybreak everyone is down at Legacy, caffeinated, ready to start. Nutmeg cuts a huge length of rope, attaching a heavy beanbag to one end. He steps back, looking up her trunk to find a good branch. "We're gonna throw this over," he tells us, "and tie the climbing rope to it." He spots the lowest strong branch; it's probably forty feet up. "My rib is still fucked, though. Who's got a good arm?"

All the guys here are pretty skinny. Stone is so loud on the bus, the boss of everyone; here he just kicks at the ground, trying to look cool, hanging back, blending in. But Jeff pipes up: "I can throw." Then he shoots me a look like, *See? I can do something too.* He hasn't volunteered for anything since we've been here. He's competing with me. I roll my eyes and look away.

Nutmeg hands the beanbag rope to Jeff. "You probably want to back way up. It's high."

Jeff nods like, *Don't tell me, dude, I know.* He backs up, winds up, and pitches. It doesn't even get close.

"Shit," he says, and I catch him glance at me, checking to see if I saw him miss. I look down instinctually. It's a habit, making sure he's not embarrassed. Like that's my job.

He tries again. Closer this time, but not by much. "God-damn it," he mutters, looking around, ears turning red under the raindrops. Everybody's watching. On the fourth try he finally gets it. It sails over the branch and swings down with a *thunk*. Stone goes, "Fuck yeah," and Jeff looks at him, puffs up a little, proud.

Nutmeg ties the throw line to the climbing rope, pulls it over and down, and then Aaron steps into a harness and ties a complicated knot, the kind of knot that someone has to teach you. He wiggles the knot up and down the main rope, making sure it moves, then clips his harness on. Exile hands him work gloves: "Wear these or it'll rip your hands up when you climb."

"Thanks," Aaron says, a little breathless, and puts them on. He looks up at the rope, hanging down from the branch, and I follow his gaze. Stretching up toward the sky, the rope looks unbelievably thin. I can't imagine how it could hold a person.

He looks at all of us. "Here goes." Sage steps forward to hug him, her fingers digging into his shoulders. I look down, cheeks flushed, feeling Jeff behind me. Aaron buries his face in her neck, unembarrassed, in front of all of us, and I wonder what it would feel like to have someone so unafraid to be with me.

And then Aaron lets go and hooks in, slips his boot into the foot loop and moves the knot up, and starts climbing.

We all watch. Five minutes and he's halfway to the branch, swaying back and forth like a monkey. The bus guys hoot and holler as he gets higher, cheering him on, like they had anything to do with it.

Ten minutes and he reaches the first branch. Forty feet up. He heaves himself onto it, hooks his harness to the tree trunk, lifts up the rope he just climbed up on, and stands to pitch it over another branch, thirty feet above his head. I've never seen anything like this. It's crazy.

"Can't he fall?" I ask.

"Not if he's harnessed in," Nutmeg says. "As long as he keeps that harness locked to a rope and his knots hold, worst that can happen is he'll dangle."

Aaron teeters on the branch as he tries to get the throw line hooked in. I don't care what Nutmeg says; harness or no harness, I'd be scared shitless to do what Aaron's doing. He's going up two hundred feet. That's where they decided he should build the platform—past the thickest branches, high enough that Cascade couldn't pull him out even if they tried.

After a while my neck starts to hurt, but I can't stop watching. Nobody can. The guys quiet down as he gets higher, and we hold our breath as he grips the rope and drags himself up, slowing down more and more the higher he gets, stopping when his strength gives out. Dirt hits my cheekbone like a raindrop, and I realize it's fallen all the way from where Aaron is, kicked off the tree. Soon I can only see him as a dot, his tan Carhartt pants bright against the dark of Legacy. The next time he stops, Exile, Sage, and Nutmeg go to the pile of gear and rope together wood, parceling it up. Goat and Bender tie rope onto a milk crate full of tools and hook a carabiner on it, then haul it over to the base of the tree. The other kids just stand around watching.

Finally Aaron hollers down to us, "Okay!" His voice

ing, deep and ragged, a kind of sound I've never heard before, and then he hits the ground, and then it stops.

We all scramble to the base of Legacy. Everything is slow motion, like in a movie; my mind feels like it's outside my body, like I'm seeing everything from above.

Sage gets there first. Ten feet away and she falls down, collapses limp onto the ground. Her wails echo through the forest, louder than any human cry I've ever heard. And I know. Nothing else could cause that sound. I know.

CHAPTER 20

I only looked for a second. I couldn't stand any longer than that; I didn't want it in my mind. The blood, the broken bones. I ran to the other side of Legacy, pressing my face against her, blacking everything out. From the other side of the tree I heard Sage, still wailing, and Nutmeg and Exile, picking Aaron up. Someone was shrieking, terrified: *What do we do? What the fuck do we do? What do we do with him?* and Exile said they had to get his body somewhere sheltered. *His body.* Five minutes earlier, he'd been *Aaron*, and just like that he was *a body*.

Then a blur, a tangle of chaos and screaming and mud, a million things, glass-sharp moments poking through the fog. When the climbers rappelled down, Jeff and Stone and Goat circled the base of Legacy: "*Murderers!*" When the climbers touched the ground, Stone's fists were swinging, his limbs a blur of fight and fury, eyes red with rage. I think he would've tried to strangle them if someone hadn't held him back.

I was staring at the climbers, thinking, *That is what a killer looks like.* They wouldn't look at us: gazes off to the side, hard and flat as rocks. "Fatality," I heard one of them say into his walkie-talkie; then, "Accidental. No injuries on this end." The other voice came through, crackly: "Shame. Well, get yourself back to base. Accidents happen out in the woods."

When we heard the engines later, we first thought *cops.* We scrambled to the dragons to lock down, braced to get arrested or worse. My heart throbbed, but I was numb: a night in jail almost felt like a relief. Escape. No choices, no decisions, no one to talk to, just flat concrete walls and a closed-off space and silence.

But then we saw: it was the coroner. They told us the death was being ruled an accident, so there wouldn't be an investigation. Then they asked for Aaron's parents' phone number.

Then they took him away.

When the numb wears off, my whole body starts sweating. I feel like I might puke again, and Exile and Nutmeg are staring daggers at Jeff, Goat, and Dirtrat, saying they provoked this, that if they hadn't gotten the other loggers so far away with their whole stunt, maybe the other loggers would've stopped those two from going up, and Jeff is arguing back that they didn't do shit, that it took planning to go up in that tree, the other loggers wouldn't have stopped anything, and Dirtrat's saying, "Know your enemy, assholes," and Cyn is hanging on to Jeff and calling Exile naïve, and Sage is yelling, "Shut *up*! Stop fucking *arguing*! Somebody's *dead*!" I can't be here. I have to be by myself. I have to get away.

I can't go back on the main trail to Legacy, so I take the other one, the one that goes back to where Jeff and I saw the deer. It seems like another lifetime when that happened. I run down the trail as fast as I can, impact shoving the breath out of my body with each step. My feet hurt as they hit the ground; I push my body harder than it's meant to go, trying to force this out of myself, like if I punish myself hard enough, I can get rid of this somehow. I'm flying down a hill, and suddenly I hit a root and wrench my ankle, pain shooting hot through my leg, and fall.

I could get up if I wanted to, but I don't try. Sobs take me over, racking my ribs, and I cry so hard it hurts, right onto the rough ground, dirt sticking to my face. There's nowhere to put this. Nowhere to go. I'm staring into a black hole of nothing but hurt, a chasm that can never close, this *wrong* against the whole of everything that can never be made right. This whole thing, this stupid camp I gave up my whole stupid life for, it's all a fucking waste. It killed someone. It did the opposite of what it was supposed to. There was no together, no fixing anything, nobody looking out for anyone making sure that things were safe, just all of us, cut loose, with nothing to protect us, not protecting each other. I can't believe this happened. My brain says *no no no no* even as I know that won't do anything, can't reverse this, there's nothing I can do. And suddenly I'm fourteen, in my room, phone ringing upstairs past eleven at night, hearing my dad say, *Who's calling so late?* and *Hello?* and then screaming *NO!* guttural, raw, the same sound as Sage at the tree. When I heard his voice, I knew. I knew and my throat went dry and my gut went sick and the room around me spun and I knew I had to lock the truth inside of me forever. I knew that I could never tell: that Andy was drunk, that I'd seen it, that I didn't stop him. That I didn't go along. If I'd gone with him, if I'd had the guts to get into that car, I could have at least made him pull over if he swerved. I could have watched his driving. I could have fixed it. But I didn't, and now the world was backward, upside down, everything opposite and wrong, and he was gone, and it would never, ever be the same again. I sob and sob, trying to empty it out, that night and today and every time I was afraid and didn't do a fucking thing, didn't say anything, didn't take a stand, but it just keeps coming and there's always more inside, more guilt, more pain, more anger, and it doesn't go away. I sob until my face hurts and my muscles are too limp to cry anymore and then I just lie there, the rawness turning to a hollow throb that I know will be inside of me forever.

At the fire that night, we're all in shock. We just sit there, staring into the orange and blue, watching the wood burn. I don't look at anyone. I watch the flame till I see spots. A spark hits my face and I don't even brush it away; I just let it burn me. Sage is beside me. Sometimes she starts crying; then eventually it subsides and she's quiet again. She doesn't talk.

Finally Exile takes his cap off, runs his hand through his dark hair, and speaks up. "I'm sorry, everybody. I know nobody wants to think about this; I know none of us can hardly even think at all." People pull their eyes off the fire and look at him. "But the reason they came to pull Aaron out today is that they're gonna cut. And no matter how it happened"—he swallows a lump in his throat—"he's out of the tree. That means Cascade can come in."

Who even cares anymore, I want to say. The voice is angry in my head, like a stubborn, pissed-off kid. *It doesn't matter. We can't stop them. The people in charge are trying to make money. That's all they want to do. The cops are helping them. There's no one to protect us; there's no one to protect anything. And we've just proved we're too small to protect it ourselves. We should just give up.*

"And the thing is," Exile goes on, "they have another reason to move fast now."

"What do you mean?" Nutmeg asks.

"Well, the cops and rangers who've come up here are all working with Cascade; that alliance is pretty tight. But someone dies, sometimes the family hires a lawyer right away, or a good cop gets curious, starts sniffing around. Anyone who might want to try to make this a crime scene and look into what happened won't be able to do that if everything gets logged. The company and the cops and rangers who are working with them are gonna want to clean this all out as fast as they can."

Shit.

Exile looks at us. "We have to block off the road. Probably tonight."

We all just look at each other. If it's about Aaron, letting them erase him, letting them pretend what happened didn't happen, it's not so easy to give up.

But none of us can even bear to think about it. Planning, solving problems: it feels impossible. And nobody trusts anybody. There's a long, long pause, where no one wants to talk.

Then, finally, Jeff looks at me, then everyone. "Okay," he says simply. "I'll head it up. Who's coming with me? I need at least five."

Exile and Nutmeg look at Jeff. I do too. Every time he's volunteered to do something here, it's been for selfish reasons. To compete with Aaron or with me; to get in with Stone, show off, make me feel like I'm a coward. I don't trust him. Not at all. Not anymore.

I stare straight at his face, right at his eyes, boring through to see what's behind them. "I'm not going to do anything stupid," Jeff says. "Or dangerous. Or anything that would piss off Cascade or the cops. Okay? I get it. It isn't time for that. Not now." He looks at Goat and Dirtrat. "Nothing dangerous, nothing risky," he tells them, and it's almost like he's giving them an order, and they nod, listening. The rest of the bus kids do too. Stone tags it: Jeff's the one they're listening to now. He's okay with it. Stone nods too.

Jeff turns back to Exile and Nutmeg. "I mean it. I'm volunteering to lock down and block the road. I get it. I know that's what we need to do."

Sage picks up her head to look Jeff in the eye. "Don't fuck with us," she says, her voice exhausted but firm, mustering the last bit of strength she can.

"You heard Exile. He's right. We need to do this," Jeff says, not backing down. "You want to stop me? I'll listen to you. But you do that, it leaves us all exposed, and it lets them cover up whatever they want to. You want to let them do that, or you want to let me take care of it?"

She doesn't answer.

"I'm trying to do something to help."

I stare at him hard, assessing him. There's nothing else behind his eyes. No bravado, no bullshit, no jealousy. His eyes are honest. Like when we used to be together in his basement, or in the tent those very first nights here, before all of this. When I still knew him. He looks like the person that I knew.

Sage looks at him a long moment, and then she finally nods.

Jeff gathers Bender and Stone, Goat and Dirtrat, Naya and Cyn; he grabs water and their gear, and waits for them to follow him. As they're about to go, he stands and looks at me. I don't know what it means. Something like, *I know that I can't fix the things that happened, but at least I can do this.*

The rest of us stay by the fire; nobody wants to be alone. We're gonna be awake all night, I can tell. Nutmeg gets Sage some food. She doesn't want to eat, but he makes her. I can't even imagine how she must feel right now. It seems like too much for one person to hold. But she is: she's sitting up, and eating, taking one breath, then another.

After a minute, some life comes back into her eyes. "Thanks," she says to Nutmeg, I guess for making her eat. "You guys mind if I go talk to Alison for a minute?" she asks the rest of the group, and they shake their heads: of course not. "C'mon," she says to me, quiet, and I help her stand up, following her to I don't know where.

She brings me to her tent and turns a lantern on. It's a mess in here, her pack pulled apart, clothes strewn everywhere. From when I came to get the camera. I made this mess when he was still alive, and now here it is, reminding us.

"Sorry," I say, and I start cleaning up her things.

"It's okay," she says. I don't stop, though. I have to put it back like it was before.

"It's okay, Alison," she says again, but I can't stop. I have to put it back.

She tugs at me. "Sit." I'm still cleaning. "C'mon. Sit down." Her voice is firm, and it snaps me out of what I'm doing. I finally stop folding.

"Listen," she says, her eyes shot through with red. "I need something from you, Alison. I need your help."

I look at her, no idea what I could possibly do that could help anything.

"I need you to help me get everyone out of here."

At first I think I must have misheard her. I just stare.

"It's pointless," she says. "Without the sit, it's just a matter of time."

I was thinking those things, just an hour ago, at the fire. But it's a whole other thing to hear her say them. It seems wrong.

"But we can stop them—we can lock down—that's what the dragons are for—"

"They'll get us out. Beat us up, pepper spray, whatever. If they want to get us out, they'll get us out." She says it matter-of-factly, like it's obvious. "I'm just being realistic," she says. "It's done. They're coming. Okay? It's safer for everyone if we just admit it's over."

She's supposed to be the one who believes. She's the one I'm supposed to look to when I don't, when I want to give up. She's not supposed to be saying this. And when she does, I really see it being over. Nobody believes. There's no hope to hold on to. I think about those clear-cuts on the highways, naked and barren; I imagine this forest turning into that, another death. Like Aaron, again, except worse, because it makes his death a waste. I feel myself getting sucked into the black hole that's inside me. *It's hopeless*, I hear myself think. *It's over. It's all bullshit.* The words in my head are the same as at the fire, but the feeling is different. It's not a temper tantrum, not stubborn frustration; it's deeper, and bigger, and bottomless. It's familiar, this place: it's all I thought there was, for years. After Andy died, till I came here, it was my life. *Maybe that's how it is. That black hole is what's real. Nothing else.*

And then suddenly I start crying. Like really crying, the kind you can't control. My chest heaves; there's snot and everything. Somewhere in the back of my mind I feel like it's selfish. It's not fair of me when Sage is here; I need to be the strong one. But I can't help it. The force of it scares me: from a place deeper and bigger than anything I recognize, anything with words, anything I've felt in years. I feel like a little kid.

I cry and cry till it feels like there's no water left in my body, till my head throbs and my eyes are sore.

Sage watches me a long time before she speaks. Finally she just asks: "Is it Aaron?"

I shake my head through the tears. That's part of it, but not all of it.

"Is it what I just said?"

It is, but it's also so much more than that. It's everything. I finally say, "I had a brother."

And then I catch myself: She just lost her boyfriend. Like *just now*. She doesn't need to hear about my bullshit problems. "Sorry," I say. "Forget it."

"No," she says slowly. "It's okay."

"He died," I start, and I'm crying again before it's even all the way out of my mouth. "This is stupid."

"It's okay," she says. "You can tell me." And I can't help it. I'm too exhausted to do anything but tell the truth. All the secrets press past my skin, and I just let them. "He was in an accident," I say. "I was fourteen. He was driving. I knew he was drunk when he was leaving, I knew it wasn't safe. I should've said something, but I didn't. I thought his friends would laugh at me. I didn't want to be embarrassed—so fucking selfish. If I'd been in the car, I could've stopped it, I could've taken the wheel or made him pull over or something. But I just let him go. Like a fucking idiot. I never told anybody. I could've stopped him." I start crying again. "I could've stopped him." I sob. "It's my fault." And then the crying takes over, and all I can say, over and over, is *It's my fault.*

"I know how you feel," she says.

And we just look at each other, together in this black hole of guilt that's bigger than us both, and for what?

"That's why I want to cut our losses," she says. "It's enough people getting hurt. You know? If you'd stopped your brother that night, if I'd stopped Aaron . . ." She trails off. "People would still be here."

But her eyes are far away; there's something distant in them. I don't think she believes what she's saying. She doesn't look like the Sage who strode up to me the first day here, who taught me how to haul water and split wood. Right now, she looks broken. I know what that looks like.

"It sucks," she says. "But it's the best that we can do."

And then I realize. The clarity cuts like a knife through the muck and sludge.

"No," I say. "It's not."

She looks up at me. "What, you have a better idea?"

I can't believe I'm going to say it.

But I do.

"I'll go up."

She looks at me, shocked. "Alison. You can't."

"Why not?" What do I have to lose? I dropped out of school. My mom will never talk to me again. Jeff's done. All I have is right here, in front of me. It might not do anything. They might be stronger than us. But I can try.

"You don't know how to climb."

"Nobody here knows how to climb."

"You're not even eighteen—I can't let you—"

"You said it yourself. If we give up on the sit, they'll just come in and cut. Then all of this is wasted."

"It's probably wasted anyway."

"But you don't know that," I say. Out on a limb, not sure if I believe myself. But there's nobody else to believe. I can feel it, the space inside me: there's nobody above me telling me what to think or how the world works, nobody making the rules. Right now, right here, what I believe is up to me. I can believe it's wasted, over, meaningless, or I can believe there's something I can do that still has a chance at changing things.

She looks at me, grave. "You're a kid. I can't have it on my shoulders. Not two of you."

"It's not on your shoulders," I say. "I'm choosing it."

She shakes her head.

I don't know for sure that it will change a thing. But I know not doing it means giving up; it means letting them win, it means the people on top who aren't protecting anything get to come in and burn it all down and for sure, definitely, there will be no one there to stop them. I know, now, that letting that happen would be a choice. That I make.

"Look," I say, a clarity coming through me that's unfamiliar, that seems to come from somewhere else, like I'm not quite planning what I'm saying, I'm just saying it. "I haven't known what I actually wanted since my brother died. I never even knew what it felt like to know what I wanted. I want to do this." I wipe my eyes and push through. "If we give up, Aaron died for nothing. I can't let it be for nothing. Not again."

She looks at me.

"Please," I say. It's dangerous, but if I don't do it, it means doing nothing, and that means I'll be dead inside anyway. "I have to."

I let it hang there, waiting. She stares at the tent floor, her clothes and Aaron's; she buries her face in her dirty hands.

And after a long, long time, she looks up, eyes clear, something sparking through, and she says, "Thank you."

CHAPTER 21

I stay in Sage and Aaron's tent all night. It's weird, being there with his stuff: sometimes Sage will look at a sweatshirt of his, or a hat, and start crying. But she doesn't want to be alone. She goes back and forth between sobbing and seeming fine. I remember that feeling from when Andy died; I feel it now, too. Like you're staring down a long dark tunnel of something that's too big to understand, and sometimes it's just normal, and other times it knocks you on your ass and you can't do anything but cry. I can't believe Aaron is gone. Just like that. I was listening to his voice, trying to find a way to help him, and then he fell, and he was gone.

The night goes on longer than most nights do, until finally the sky turns indigo, and then the sunrise starts. Watching the light turn yellow out the tent flap, I get that adrenaline feeling of up all night: wrung out, dried up, exhausted and awake at the same time. And I realize: now I'm not going up in Legacy "tomorrow" anymore; I'm going up "today."

I need to stretch out the next couple of hours as long as I can. I lie there beside Sage, listening to her breathe; she finally fell asleep. Aaron probably lay here like this sometimes, staring at this ceiling, inhaling this air, waiting for her to wake up. Now that she's sleeping, I can finally feel the quiet parts of what I feel: his absence carving a hole in me, leaving me unprotected from the outside, too, both sides of my skin surrounded by empty. There's no one to take care of me. Not Aaron, not Andy, not my mom or my dad. Not Jeff, not Sage. It's just me. That's all I've got. I feel naked, like a baby, like I need to be taken care of, and at the same time I feel more grown-up than I ever have. Like I have to take care of myself. I'm going to have to. There's no one here but me.

When Sage wakes up, we walk to the kitchen. Nutmeg and Exile are there, making oatmeal for everyone. As soon as they see Sage, they all stop what they're doing.

There's this strange power in being the closest person to someone who just died. Everyone defers to you, looks after you, like a queen or a baby; you're the most powerful person in the room, because you're the most broken. It happened with my mom: at Andy's funeral everyone surrounded her, tending to her, bringing her things, asking what she needed. My dad, my grandparents, all their friends. It made me mad. Andy was my family, too; I lost him too, and nobody was gathering around me. It wasn't fair. I hated everyone for it, and I hated my mom most of all.

But now I see: the closest person does need the most. It seems natural for us to take care of Sage, even though all of us are hurting. And it's not her fault. I think of my mom. She was the closest. I see a little more of what it might have been like, and a tiny space of forgiveness opens up inside me. Just a little crack, as thin as a sliver, so small, but enough for the light to get in.

"It's basically all set up already," Sage says as she gathers gear for me. "Everything you'll need, a sleeping bag, the platform. I mean, I think it is. I don't know if there was any damage done when . . ." She can't finish that sentence.

"The climbers might've damaged the platform," Nutmeg jumps in, saving Sage. "So we're gonna send some scrap wood in your pack, in case you have to patch anything. There's a hammer up there. Just try to reinforce it so it's strong."

"Fingers crossed the mobile phone's okay," Exile says. "If you can't find it, let us know right away; someone will have to drive to the city and get one. That's the most important thing; that's how you'll get the word out."

"Get the word out about what?"

"About Aaron," Nutmeg says. "And what happened yesterday."

A fresh wave of panic prickles my skin. I didn't realize

I was supposed to talk to people. Not about that. The idea paralyzes me. "Wait—who am I calling? What am I supposed to say?"

"Aaron'll have a list of numbers up there," Exile says, and then stumbles. "I mean, there should be one that Aaron had." Pain flashes across his pale face and he looks down. "Sorry."

"It's okay," Sage says, taking over. "All our contacts should be written down. Call Pacific Land Protection Council; they can help get the word out, and they'll know how to deal with the media. Ask them for advice. It's okay to tell them you don't know how to do it all."

I'm not used to asking strangers for help. But I guess if Aaron knew them, they're not strangers.

"And then just start going down the list," Nutmeg says. "Most of the other people on it are friends, organizers, other activists and stuff. Explain to them that Cascade is gonna pull out all the stops to get in here to log this week. They want that 'accidental death' ruling to stand—otherwise they could be charged, if someone wants to charge them—and if they level this forest, there won't ever be any evidence to question whether it was an accident. If we can keep the space protected just a little longer, they can't cut. So: everybody needs to come. We need an influx of people from everywhere. Seattle, Tacoma, Eugene, Portland, Humboldt—everyone who can should get here, now."

"Okay." I nod. I don't think I've ever talked to that many people in my life. I have no idea whether I can do this. But I guess I have to try.

My bag is packed, my gear stashed in a milk crate, and they've got the ropes together. Nutmeg is about to help me get the harness on. Then the only thing left to do is climb.

Everyone keeps telling me it'll be okay, even though we all know for damn sure it might not. I'm doing it, though. I have to. It's the only thing I can do that's good. And I have to do something good. I know what the alternative is. I've spent too long living there already.

But one more thing is nagging at me, and right before I put the harness on, I finally realize what it is: Jeff. Whoever he's turned into, whatever he did, whatever he thinks of me now—whatever I think of him—I knew him once, really knew him. I have to say goodbye.

"Go fast," Sage and Exile say. "We'll wait here." I can tell they're nervous that something will happen to keep me from climbing: Jeff will talk me out of it or Cascade will show up, or cops. But they let me go.

"Hurry back, okay?" Nutmeg yells after me, and I holler back, "I will."

I skid down the trail to the front lines, going as fast as I can. Twenty feet away and I can see them, still locked down, lying in a human chain across the road. As much as I can't stand those guys, I'm proud of what they're doing. It's the right thing. And Jeff was the one who made it happen, even though it wasn't his idea. Because he knew it needed to. He's making the same choice I am. No matter what, at least we still have that in common.

When I get a little closer, they hear my footsteps, and they turn to look. "What are you doing here? What happened?" Jeff asks. I see worry in everyone's eyes.

"Everyone's okay," I say. "Nobody's hurt." Shoulders relax back into the dirt. I come around in front of Jeff. "Can I talk to you?"

"What do you need?"

"I need to talk to you," I say. "Can you unlock?"

He hesitates. "I don't know if that's a good idea. It'll leave a gap . . ."

"Jeff," I say. "I'm going up in the tree. Right now."

He stares at me, incredulous. "You're going up?"

"I have to." I nod, sober. "Walk with me?"

At first we don't talk; neither of us knows what to say. Too much has happened, too many things we haven't talked about. It's hard to know where to start.

Finally he cuts the silence. "So, you're going up."

"Yeah." I'm not sure what else to say. I just keep walking.

"How come?" He stuffs his fists into his pockets. His eyes are soft.

"Someone has to," I tell him. "The blockade at the road

isn't enough to keep them from coming in. I mean," I scramble, old habits dying hard, "not that it isn't important."

He looks at me, and I can tell he saw me scramble. He can see that thing I'm doing, that I've always done, making myself just a little smaller so that he won't feel bad. He doesn't say anything, but it passes between us.

"Why is it you?" he asks.

I don't want to lie anymore. I told the truth last night, about Andy: the hardest thing, the most shameful thing, the thing I thought would always be a secret. And the world didn't end. That pressure on the inside of my skin, all my stacked-up secrets, finally dissolved. I feel light now—scared, but strong.

I don't want to go back to how I was.

"I have to," I say.

He just looks at me, waiting for more. It's opposite of how it used to be: now I'm the one who's supposed to do the talking; he's the one listening.

"Since Andy died—I don't know . . ." I trail off.

It's harder to tell Jeff. With Sage, it just came tumbling out. But he keeps looking at me. Waiting.

"I guess since then I've thought the world just sucked, that there was nothing I could do."

"Yeah," he says, nodding, brow furrowed, understanding.

"But now there's something I can do. You know? I don't know if it'll work. It could be pointless. But I have to at least try."

We walk for a minute, not talking.

"Are you scared?" he finally asks.

"Scared shitless." I crack a smile.

"I probably would be too."

"Are you kidding? You definitely would," I rib him.

I worry for a second that I went too far, but then he smiles back.

"Yeah, for sure," he admits.

There's another silence, the air swelling up to full between us, and then he says, "It's cool of you."

"Thanks."

"No, I'm serious. It's super-brave. I don't know if I could do it." He looks at me, real respect in his eyes. Admiration, even.

I look back. "It's just the right thing."

"Lots of people feel that and they still don't do it."

I think I used to be that kind of person.

"Yeah."

He's quiet for a minute, walking. Then he asks, "Do you need anything?"

I used to need so many things from him.

I'm quiet for a minute too. "I think I'm good," I say, and it's the truth.

Finally he leans in, awkward, like he's not sure whether to kiss me or shake my hand or pat me on the back. His shoulder brushes against me, clumsy, and I just grab him and give him a hug, a real one, not like things used to be, just what makes sense, in this one moment, now.

CHAPTER 22

I stand at the base of Legacy, harnessed in, ropes hung, knots tied. I watch myself do everything I watched Aaron do a week ago: check the knots, put the gloves on, stare up the trunk. He must have felt so tiny, seeing how far he had to scale, taller than a building, him a little dot at the bottom. Nutmeg shows me how to climb, slide the knot up, hook your foot in—how to stabilize the knot so I can dangle and rest when I need to.

"Make sure you take breaks if you get tired. It's safer," he says. I hug him and Exile goodbye, then Sage. Afterward she pulls back, her hands on my shoulders, and stares into my eyes. "I bet your brother would be proud."

Thirty feet off the ground and my arms are shaking so much I can hardly hang on, let alone keep going. I can't believe how hard it is. I'm afraid to let go, but my arms are giving out; I don't have a choice. I steady the knot; then I unclench my hands.

At first I hold my breath, but the harness holds me and I dangle, swaying. I'm scared to look down, but I can't help it. It's far, far enough to make my head spin, but they're down there, watching, and my harness holds, and after a minute I relax. When I do, the adrenaline clenched in my muscles floods through my veins. I climb again.

The branches get closer together as I go up and up and up, needles scratching my cheeks, face close to her trunk, nothing except me and the branches and the rope and the bark. The rest of the world falls away as I focus, sweat streaming into my eyes, every muscle working. When I stumble, there's a branch there; when my hand slips, there's a knot. Like something bigger than me, watching out for me. It almost feels like the tree's listening to me, even though I know that's impossible. Or maybe I'm listening to her.

By the time I'm almost at the platform, I feel like I know her as well as I've ever known a person. Like we've been through something together. I take one last break and wrap my arms around her trunk, resting on my harness, breathing in the smell of dirt and pine and sap.

Then I get ready for what's next.

The platform is a mess. Aaron's gear was tied in so it couldn't fall, but it got knocked around bad. I feel like I'm on a TV show, or in a movie: *This is a crime scene. Someone died.*

You can see the outlines of what happened: there's a big empty space where they were fighting, all Aaron's stuff shoved to the sides. Buckets, milk crates, books, knocked over and tossed. One of the blue tarps hung above the platform is half torn down, flapping like an empty plastic bag in the wind. I see the concrete lockbox attached to the trunk, and I realize that's the thing that Aaron was trying to lock to. When he unhooked his harness. When he fell. I don't want to look at it. But I know I have to: I need to know how it works in case they send someone up here after me.

I drink some water from the jug that Exile and I sent up to him that afternoon, and then I start cleaning.

I'm not going to let this platform become what my mom made Andy's room. I'm not leaving everything how it was to make sure I don't dislodge a tiny fragment of his memory. Memory is a living thing, something that changes. Aaron would want me to keep it alive, not trap it in his *stuff*.

I wipe up spills, put food in one place, tools in another. I find the flashlight, and the phone, and the solar charger: they're all here. Everything I touch, I think, *He just touched this. Yesterday.* Like some part of him is left on it, his fingerprints or breath. It's so strange, how someone can be here, and then they're gone. I don't think I'll ever understand it.

I pour water on a rag and kneel to clean the platform floor. I'm scrubbing mud off the edges when I see the blood. And it hits me: he was hurt. Whatever happened up here, whether it was an accident or not—he was hurt. Before he fell, and during; the last thing his body felt was pain.

And that's what makes me finally crack. Aaron would never hurt anything. He never even got mad. It's just so fucking *unfair*.

It wells up in me, a hot mix of anger and sadness, and I punch the platform. It hurts my hand; the hurt feels good. I punch it again, and then again, and then I just start pounding, not caring that it shakes beneath me, not caring that I'll have to fix it if it breaks. I just want something to hit. That platform becomes everything: the climbers who took Aaron, the car that took Andy, everyone who ever hated me at school. Andy's friends after he died, all the guys who hit on me without caring who I was. My dad for leaving. My mom for leaving *me*. Myself. I pound till my fists hurt, till my shoulders move past achy to weak, till the mad drains away and all that's left is tired. I lie there, spent, empty, and I say to the sky, *Okay. I don't know what else there is. Just fill me up.*

When I wake up, the sun's an hour lower in the sky. I sit up and rub my eyes and look around, and for the first time I see where I am. You can see for miles, forest carpeting the mountains, fields in the distance, clouds and sky. And here and there, dotting the sides of hills, bare and dry, are the clear-cuts. Brown patches in the midst of green, death in the middle of life. And not the good kind of death: not the kind that comes when it's time, when you've lived out your life and you circle back. The kind that comes too early. From something that shouldn't happen. Like a chain saw. Or a climber. Or a car. Like someone dying, and your life falling apart, and getting caught in the deep muck of darkness and despair. That's why I'm up here. To fight *that*.

I plug the phone into the solar charger and I start calling. I do what Sage says, start with PLPC, even though I don't feel qualified to talk to them. I do it anyway. It's fine. They'll send a press release out. They don't bite. I don't fuck up.

Late the next morning Sage and Exile come with a milk crate full of water and food. They holler; I look down and see them, two tiny dots on the ground. I can't believe I'm so high up. "Lower the rope!" Sage yells. I do, and she hooks the crate on. "Now pull it up!" Hand over hand, I raise the crate up two hundred feet.

Inside is a jug of water, a box of food, and a note. *Almost twenty new people last night and this morning! They heard from PLPC. We're gonna try to surround the area as much as possible. There's enough people here now that we actually have a chance. THANK YOU. Are you okay up there? Love, Sage.*

I wish I was down there. I want to be with all those people, helping, instead of up here, alone with myself. I want to be with everyone, even the strangers, part of the world instead of scared of it. Up here, there's only me and the quiet. It's lonely. But it's where I have to be. I rip a page from Aaron's notebook. *Yeah, I'm good.*

After a while the calls get easier. I know what to say: I don't have to think about it every time. You just tell the truth, over and over, until it doesn't scare you anymore. Like splitting wood, or digging ditches: after a while you just know how to do it. Nobody taught me this. I taught myself.

I make coffee with the solar hot plate, eat from containers of dried fruit, climb up a couple branches when my muscles start cramping up. When I'm waiting between calls, I lean in close to Legacy, feeling her beside me, huge and majestic and alive. I watch squirrels hop on branches above me, birds build nests and carry food. Ferns sprout from moss on the crooks of the branches, and there is so much life here, in this one tiny place, and when I look out on the forest, the parts that aren't cut, I see how much life there is everywhere, as long as we let it keep living. We all have empty spaces inside us. I have holes in me from Andy, from my dad, my mom, from Aaron now. It's normal to try to make them go away. That's what I did forever: sex with Andy's friends, getting high with Jeff, being pissed off at my mom. Everybody does it: we try to fill the holes inside us with cars and thoughts and toys and plastic stuff, things to control and things to buy, and *that's* what kills things. If we would just let those empty spaces be, all this living air would rush into them. It's all around us. I breathe in deep.

That night the wind whips the platform hard. In the forest the trees shelter you; in the city, walls do. Here, there's nothing: besides the tarps rattling above my head, I'm completely exposed. I swear the winds are faster this high up. I huddle down in Aaron's sleeping bag, wrapped in wool sweaters, still freezing. Legacy sways, sending me sliding on the platform until I shorten my rope and hook my harness in tighter, hugging her trunk. I hang on to her for dear life. My harness holds.

The next day there's more people at the Free State, and more the next. Sometimes I can hear their voices drift up, laughter and singing and the sounds of hard work. Someone brings a dog; I hear it barking. I learn to hang on tight while I'm sleeping, keep myself warm, talk myself down when the winds get too high. And every day when the sun rises, I clean up the debris from the night before, stack and straighten everything before I make my Folgers instant, my own little morning ritual, like an adult.

Today I'm cleaning the platform, sun rising orange through a pink sky, when I realize this won't be forever. Whether we win or we don't, whatever happens, this will end. I won't have a platform to clean, a sleeping bag to roll. I'll have to make my coffee on the ground. It'll feel good:

running water, showers, towels, electricity at night. A bed. I can't wait to sleep in a bed. But then I realize: I have no idea where that bed will be.

And my heart starts racing.

I threw it all away. For two months I've been hiding from that, pressing it down, elbowing it out of my mind, distracting myself. I dropped out of school. I ran away from my mom. I've spent all this time telling myself *she doesn't care*, but now, alone with myself, I can't keep that lie going. I know that isn't true, or at least it isn't the whole truth. The whole time I've been pushing away this dull panic, and now it forces its way through.

I look west across the mountains, and in the distance I imagine I can see Tacoma. I can't, of course; it's way too far. But if I squint hard, I can see where the buildings start, and I imagine my house that I don't know if I can go back to, the world I came from.

It's weird: for the first time, right now, when I think about my mom, I don't only feel angry. She still did everything she did. But I guess since Aaron died, I understand it more. It's hard to know what to do when in one single instant your entire world changes, the center of it just suddenly gone. It makes a vacuum at the core of you; you feel like something has to fill it or you'll stop breathing.

I always thought that she was punishing me somehow. Like somewhere inside, she knew it was my fault that Andy died, and everything that happened after was my penance. But now I'm not so sure it was my fault. It's like when Sage said, *I can't let you go up there, Alison,* and I knew it wasn't about her letting me or not. I chose to come up here. It wasn't up to her. She couldn't have stopped me, even if she tried.

Even if I could have said something, even if I should have, Andy got in that car himself. He made his own decisions. I was just fourteen; it wasn't up to me. Maybe nobody was punishing me.

Maybe all this time I've been punishing myself.

I want to tell my mom the truth. That I didn't stop him, and that it wasn't my fault. I want to tell her that I need her to get better somehow, that I can't do that work for her. That I'll never replace him. That I'll never fill that space in her, and I shouldn't have to. That I need her to figure out how to see me, here, right now, because I'm still breathing, and I'm part of things, and things go on.

I don't know if she can do it. But I know that if she doesn't, it's not my fault.

Whatever I do after this, it doesn't have to be penance.

The next day I wake up, look at the notches I've been carving in the platform, and I realize: this is it. Today is the last day on Cascade's permit. It's the last day that they have. My heart starts pounding: if they're coming up, today's the day they'll do it. If they don't, we will have won.

I sit, high up and still, all day. I'm watching for climbers, for trucks; but I'm also memorizing it, the curves of the mountains, the slant of the hills, the way the light turns the leaves into a million shades of green. Wherever I go next, I want to take this with me.

Halfway through the day I run out of space in Aaron's old journal. I dig in my backpack, searching for some scrap of something, the back of a notebook to write down the rest of this day, and as I'm rooting through, I find it. That folded-up letter from Antioch. The edges are frayed and there's sap on one side of it—it's stained and sticky and a mess—but it's there.

I open it up. *Dear Alison: We are thrilled to invite you to join the Antioch community.* That familiar knot twists inside me—knowing someone wants me, and knowing I can never say yes. But then I think, *Never say yes.* That's what I thought before.

But I thought a lot of things before. I thought Jeff knew more than me; I thought I couldn't do anything. I thought the bad things that happened were my fault, and that the black hole was the only thing that was real. I thought I didn't want anything. That there was nothing to want. I was wrong about all of that. Maybe I'm wrong about this, too.

I don't know how it would work. There isn't money. I can't pretend that's different; that's just real. But if my mom got them to give me Andy's UCSB scholarship, maybe I could get someone to give me one of my own. To the place I want to go to. Someplace that's mine.

I unfold the pages. Smooth out the torn edges. And then

I rip the cardboard cover off of Aaron's spiral notebook, and I lay it on the platform, and I start writing. *Dear Antioch. My name is Alison. I can't afford tuition at your school, but I want to come there. I'm writing this to you from a platform on a tree. Here's why.*

I know it's midnight from the voices: a cheer from the direction of camp wakes me up. They didn't come in. They're not coming in. It's over, and we won. I sit up in the sleeping bag, look out at the sky. Stars stretch above the mountains, the horizon invisible in the darkness, everything outside me one big open thing.

My hand grips the envelope tight; it's addressed and stamped already. Tomorrow I'll take apart this platform, put my pack on, hold tight to Legacy as I scale down. I'll put my feet back on the ground. I'll keep that envelope close to me while I hug everyone here goodbye, and in town I'll find a mailbox, and after that the roads will open up in front of me, and there will be things along them that I can't imagine yet; I'll know where I want to go, and I'll make a way to get there.

ACKNOWLEDGMENTS

Nothing happens in the world without community, and *Legacy* would not have been possible without the support of countless people. My greatest thanks goes to the radical kids (and adults!) of Earth First!, who have been putting their bodies on the line since 1979 to protect the irreplaceable beauty and wildness of the earth. It's easy to take the health of the planet for granted—but we cannot survive unless nature survives, and I am grateful to the activists who put themselves on the line to protect the earth for all who inhabit it. I'm also grateful to the water protectors, #NoDAPL activists, and all Native activists who were on this land first and who continue to stand up for the health and integrity of this land in the face of almost unimaginable opposition. Thank you to the giant redwoods of Northern California, which gave me my first experience of true awe.

Thank you to David Miller, Jonathan Matthew Smucker, and the Minnehaha Free State for sparking my sense of wonder and hope way back when, as well as for your commitment, work, and ideas that continue to be crucial in the fight for the world we know is possible. Thanks also to Han Shan for that same fighting spirit and for the many research assists along the way. I deeply appreciate the support of Jen Besser and Arianne Lewin, who shepherded this book at Penguin from the time when it was just an idea, and to my agent, Joe Veltre, who has been with me since my first book. Big, beautiful thanks to my parents, Art and Donna Blank, who instilled in me from birth the understanding that we all share a responsibility to speak truth to power and co-create a more sustainable and just world. Thank you to my awesome sister, Tasha Blank, who gets all of the things this book is about, and who helped spark the idea on an epically magical forest hike. Thank you to my amazing husband, Erik Jensen, who supports me gorgeously in every single creative endeavor, and to our incredible, inspiring, fierce daughter, Sadie, who gives me something to fight for.

"Never doubt that a small group of thoughtful, committed citizens can change the world. Indeed, it's the only thing that ever has."

—Margaret Mead